Tessa
in
Love

Kate le Vann was born in Doncaster and lives in York. She has written for *CosmoGirl!*, *Vogue, Company* and *The Big Issue*, and is the author of four highly acclaimed novels for teenagers, *Tessa in Love, Things I Know About Love, Two Friends, One Summer* and *Rain*.

KATE
LE VANN

Tessa
in
Love

Piccadilly Press • London

Many thanks to Brenda Gardner, Yasemin Uçar and everyone
at Piccadilly, and to Miranda Eason, Celia Duncan and
everyone at CosmoGIRL!

This edition published 2009
First published in Great Britain in 2005
by Piccadilly Press Ltd,
5 Castle Road, London NW1 8PR
www.piccadillypress.co.uk

Text copyright © Kate le Vann, 2005

A catalogue record for this book is available from the British Library

ISBN: 978 1 84812 000 6

1 3 5 7 9 10 8 6 4 2

Printed in the UK by CPI Bookmarque, Croydon, CR0 4TD
Text design by Louise Millar
Cover design by Susan Hellard and Fielding Design
Set in StempelGaramond and Carumba

Chapter 1

'Love is the last thing we need right now, Tessa,' Matty said.

As the credits rolled, we were both in a drippy, hopeless kind of state, having laughed at the cheesiness of the movie for as long as we could, and then fallen for it anyway. As usual.

'But why?' I said loudly, sounding a bit like I was going to burst into song. 'I want it. And you're in love anyway. Lee is perfect for you and he's not going to die in a sword fight.'

'No, but . . .'

'He's seriously cute.'

'Well, yeah, but . . .'

'We spend half our time watching soppy old films and wishing our lives were like theirs and yours *is*. Without the tragedy.'

'Augghh!' Matty said, rolling over as if I was too much for her to take. We'd moved on to the carpet during the hero's death scene: the sofa was too far away from the action.

'Sorry,' I said, and shoved a handful of Maltesers in my mouth so I wouldn't be tempted to interrupt for a while.

'This year,' she said, 'Lee finishes his A-levels and we finish our GCSEs, which means serious work for both of us at the time it's most important to spend time together, and at the end of the year he'll go to university, and then two years after that maybe I will, and we have to make decisions about whether we'll have a long distance relationship or . . . you know, something else.'

'Oh,' I said.

'Oh?' she said, pretending to be annoyed. 'Is that all you've got?'

I was still sucking chewed-up Maltesers out of my teeth, to be honest, but I liked the way my hesitation sounded thoughtful and serious. 'Well . . . it is going to be difficult,' I said. I couldn't work out whether she was properly sad or just post-movie sad, but I wanted to cheer her up either way. 'But you'll make it work. You'll find ways of being together, and he'll have long holidays. I know you'll be OK. And speaking as someone who's never had any problems with romance apart from *not* having any bloody romance, I'd swap with you in a second. I'm the one who just spent Valentine's Day last week playing computer games with my little brother, whereas –

if I remember correctly – you were out with Lee being given pink roses and a crystal bracelet.'

Matty smiled dreamily and idly played with the bracelet. 'Loads of boys fancy you,' she said. 'You're just too choosy.'

Matty is so sweet – although if I looked like her I'd probably be nice to everyone and go around loving the world too. She is insanely good-looking, with this glossy reddish-mahogany bob (the colour is, admittedly, helped out a bit by L'Oréal), perfect porcelain skin and Angelina Jolie lips. And a real chest with a real C-cup, while I struggle to fill an A. My dirty-blond hair just seems to go mousy and frazzled when I try to colour it, and my skin is *im*perfect deathbed-white, and at no point in my life has there been a time when loads of boys fancied me.

But Matty always talked as if we were both pretty. When we went to parties, she'd say things like, 'I think we might just knock them dead tonight; I think jaws will drop when we walk in,' although what tended to happen with me was, I only made people's jaws drop when they yawned with boredom.

'I'm not choosy,' I said. 'I'm easy.'

'Ha ha ha ha ha!' Matty said. Then she gave me a look, that meant something like, 'I have made an excellent point and won the argument.'

'How many people have asked me out?' I sighed.

'Well,' Matty said, 'you scare them off. They think you're beautiful and unattainable . . .'

'Oh God, Matt, come *off it* . . .'

'Tessa, you do give boys a hard time!'

I *sometimes* gave boys a hard time because I knew they didn't fancy me, and by arguing with them, it was as if I was keeping a bit of self-respect. So, they might not have thought I was good-looking or sexy or fun, but I could put them straight on global warming or tell them how their super-cool trainers exploited workers in Vietnam, and kid myself that I was being clever, at least.

Well, maybe I'm being unfair to myself. What *actually* happened was, I panicked a lot. I did really try to care about what was happening in the world, and I did get frustrated that most of the people I knew never seemed to look beyond the latest designer labels and photos of celebrities with cellulite. But if I was talking to a boy I fancied and he was teasing me for not knowing about some hip band, I tried to remember how Matty would do it, the way she made arguing seem adorable and flirty, but I always ended up sounding over-serious (even though I wasn't), as if my sense of humour had been surgically removed at birth. I think boys never realised I might be joking – Matty said they sometimes told her I was quite intense. But I wasn't intense! I just . . . couldn't think of *anything* to say that wasn't really boring, so I often clammed up.

'Well, all I know is, being gorgeous never put anyone off,' I said.

'But who do you want?' Matty said. 'You haven't mentioned anyone since John Cheeseman.'

I squealed. 'Don't!'

'But you *loved* John Cheeseman!' Matty said, wickedly.

'I was in a very different "place" . . .'

'Ooh, John Cheeseman is sooo sexy,' Matty said, getting into her impression of me. 'What can I do to get John Cheeseman?'

One year before, a new boy came to our school called John Cheeseman. He was a blond and I liked blond boys, he wore glasses and I liked boys with glasses, and he seemed shy and quiet. I talked to Matty about him and she sort of got us together at a party with a bit of not very subtle hinting, and he turned out to be a) obsessed with playing Dungeons and Dragons, b) convinced he would be the youngest ever Conservative prime minister, and c) – this is the one that really mattered – the kind of boy who licks not just your tonsils when he snogs you but most of your face, up to and including your nose and down to your neck. John Cheeseman had also – the final insult! – not wanted to 'see' me after our incredibly wet snog, and spent the next week hiding behind corners when he spotted me. In a moment of incredibly out of character sassiness, and because he was one of the few people at school who was definitely less cool than me, I finally followed him round a corner and said – loudly – 'Stop running, John Cheeseman, no one is coming to get you.' For a week this was kind of a school catchphrase, which was half funny and half drop-dead embarrassing.

John Cheeseman was also the last boy I had snogged. And sort of the first. I half-heartedly fancied the same people I'd half-heartedly fancied for years, but nothing was ever going to happen with them, and I wasn't sure I really wanted it to. I wanted someone else. Someone different.

'It's too late with all the boys we know,' I said. 'They know me now. I can't pretend I'm sexy and fun.'

'It's not pretending!' Matty said, 'You are!'

'Not to *boys*!' I protested. 'I'm weird and serious. I need someone a bit geeky like me. Someone who reads newspapers rather than *FHM*.'

'Oh lord,' Matty said wearily. 'No boy our age gives a toss about newspapers.'

'Well, they should.'

'No, I tell a lie, John *Cheeseman* was *very* political . . .'

'I'm warning you, Matty . . .' I said, trying to sound serious but giggling.

'Look, the point is, first you find a boy and then you change him, but make sure you start with a cute one.'

'I don't want to change someone,' I said. 'Is it so much to ask for him to come ready-made?'

'Too. Choosy,' Matty whispered.

'Well, look,' I said, trying to get off the subject of my love life, 'You haven't changed Lee, have you?'

'Lee?' Matty said. 'The ultimate playa? I've tamed him.'

'As if anyone would look at another girl when he's got you.'

Matty looked sad for a moment. 'He looks at other girls plenty,' she said quietly. 'He talks about them too, more than I'd like.'

'Oh, boys are crap,' I said quickly. I was suddenly sad too, and ashamed of myself for not asking her enough about how things were going with Lee. I'd always assumed Matty could deal with anything.

'But Tessa, that's the point,' she said, brightening up again, because she liked giving me advice. 'Boys *are* crap. Don't wait for ever for someone who you think ticks every box – just give one a chance. Forget all this politically aware rubbish; find someone who makes you laugh, and make a move.'

'If only,' I said.

'And you have to admit, you have your shallow side,' Matty said, casually plaiting her hair so that it looked accidentally gorgeous.

I opened my mouth to protest.

'Don't even try! You love sparkly tops and boy bands and sitcom romances. What if you meet this bloke and he won't consider you because he's holding out for someone who only watches BBC2?'

'Um . . . persuade him he can change me?' I said. 'OK, OK, you're right.'

'I'm an expert in this field,' Matty said. 'I've done my research.'

I rolled my eyes, and took the next DVD out of its case: *Love Story*.

Chapter 2

'**O**h my God, can I see that?' I said, snatching the local paper out of my dad's hands.

He sat there with his hands in the same position and said, 'Do you know, I could have sworn I was holding something.'

'Sorry, Dad,' I said. 'But it's important! You know there've been plans to build a supermarket over Cadeby Wood? Well they're *doing* it, and . . .'

'Ah, Cadeby Wood,' my dad said. 'How many careless young venturers have been lost in its unfathomable depths?'

'Yeah, OK,' I said. 'But it's going to be even less of a wood soon.'

Cadeby Wood had been a big, dense wood when I was really tiny. Matty and I used to collect little branches there and make them into witches' broomsticks at Hallowe'en, and there were bluebells in the spring and wild strawberries in the summer, and Matty's first boyfriend, Jim Fisk, had carved 'James Lvs Matilda' on a tree with a craft-knife and cut his hand doing it. But as we grew bigger, the wood got smaller: in the last five or six years, housing estates had started to eat away at it on all sides. Now it was just a quite big patch of trees and rocks between two estates, but everyone still called it the Wood, even though, like now in the winter, you could see through to the other side of it and no one who walked in a straight line for more than ten minutes could get lost in it. But there were still rabbits, and woodpeckers and I'd seen foxes there, and it still upset me that a supermarket was going to destroy the last bits of it that were still hanging on, just to open their millionth branch when there were plenty of other supermarkets in the area. Another real thing would be lost to another ugly man-made clone building, but they'd tell you it was about providing more choice.

'It *is* bad news,' my mum said, looking over my shoulder at the paper. 'There'll be queues of cars coming in and out of the car park right into the evening. This is a residential area. That's such a dangerous idea. There are children playing in the street, cats . . .'

'The bad news is, no more vaguely illegal bonfires,' my brother Jack said.

'Have you and your stupid friend Hoxton been starting fires again?' Mum asked.

'I'm kidding,' Jack replied, looking shifty.

'If you come in with a burned-black coat again, I'm

not buying you a new one,' she said, glaring at him.

'The good news is,' Jack went on, 'supermarkets mean only one thing: *skate park*!'

'Oh no . . .' Mum said.

'I can't believe you're pleased about this,' I said. I loved my brother, but he was shallower than a saucer of water.

'Hey, I'm not pleased about it,' Jack said. 'I'm just one of those people who always sees the positive side.' He blew his nose really loudly.

'I'm so depressed,' I said. 'It's an area of outstanding natural beauty.'

The rest of my family exchanged looks, as if I was out of my tree. 'Oh, you lot just don't know how to look at things!'

'So go and join the protest,' Jack said. 'There's a tree-hugging party there on Saturday. Chain yourself to a trunk.'

'I think it was a *newspaper* . . .' my dad said, holding up his hands in the same position again. 'Yes, I think I was holding a *newspaper*.'

'Sorry,' I said, giving it back. 'Here.'

Instant Message with Matty Prentiss
<mattyjp@spectraweb.com>
5.17 p.m.

Tessa in Love

tessataylor: can you believe neelson's supermarket is really being built over cadeby wood?

mattyjp: um . . . what a shame?

tessataylor: v v v v depressed about it. they will kill the foxes and animals that live there, you know — with BULLDOZERS.

mattyjp: that so-called wood is so tiny now anyway. there're no foxes there any more. look, it is sad but they'll do World Exclusive Mara Uris make-up range if it opens there. it is v cheap and lovely. bought it in big branch in Manchester once.

tessataylor: can't believe you're not more upset. what time are you eating? come and meet me there for a min, have another look at your love tree, feel nostalgic for your youth, then angry.

mattyjp: ha! love tree. If u had john cheeseman tree u would be the first on the bulldozer.

tessataylor: i would not turn my nose up at a tree carved in my honour and leave it to be cut down.

mattyjp: mum says tea nearly ready, also have
to do physics homework now because EastEnders
wedding is tonight followed by documentary about
breast reduction. and it's FREEZING out there!

tessataylor: so wear a hat. five minutes, oh
go on please? want to talk. also just so
bored, need to get out of house.

mattyjp: OK see u outside mine, soon.

tessataylor: thanks, you're a star.

'You want me to come here *again*?' Matty said, retying
her scarf around her neck. It was cold and getting dark,
and we were both wearing woolly hats, except she looked
adorable in hers and I looked silly in hats.

'Yeah, Saturday, I mean tomorrow, there's like an
official protest thing.'

'Well, just bring me back something to sign.'

'Don't you want to go?' I said. 'Here –' I showed her
the notice, which was tacked to an oak tree.

'Where *is* the James Lvs Matilda tree, anyway?'
Matty said. 'It's been ages since I saw it.'

I walked her through, knowing the exact place
because it was near to a really interesting white, dead
skeleton tree that I loved. Jim's carving was really faint

and the 'a' at the end of Matilda was badly cut, because Jim had realised he was bleeding too much to take his time but really wanted to finish.

Jim was actually still nuts about Matty, but he pretended he just wanted to be her friend now. Secretly, I had always liked Jim more than Lee, and even fancied him a bit, but I knew he'd always fancy Matty and I'd only ever be his second choice.

'Hmm.' Matty laughed softly. 'I bet Jim would die if he knew this was still here.'

'Jim knows it's still here,' I said.

'I don't know – he moved ten miles away. I shouldn't think he visits the wood much any more.'

'Well, maybe.'

'Jim's sweet. I should tease him about it.'

I had no idea how Matty had the confidence to laugh at the idea of anyone fancying her, as if it wasn't a really big deal. Poor Jim. He'd love it, though; he loved it when Matty showed him *any* interest.

'Yikes, scary boy!' I said, jumping when I saw a tall kid with long shaggy hair and an army-green coat approaching us. 'It's OK – there are two of us,' I said, my heartbeat still quite fast.

'Tessa, we don't have to be scared of boys – we're women now,' Matty said.

'Well *you* are,' I said, thinking of her chest.

'What's up, girls?' the boy said, coming closer. 'Saying goodbye to the trees while you still have a chance?'

'Mm,' Matty said, and I just made a little squeaky noise. He smiled and slowed down as if he might stop and talk, but then he carried on walking past us.

'What was that noise I made?' I said, cringing. The boy had his hands in his pockets and walked with a bit of a sexy sway. He didn't look back at us.

'You're so easily scared,' Matty said.

'I think he goes to our school, doesn't he?'

'Yes,' Matty said.

'He's got a weird name,' I said. 'It's like Shaggy or Catman or something . . .'

'Wolfie.'

'Or Griff . . . oh yeah, Wolfie. Do you know him?'

'He was a friend of Mudassar,' Matty said. Mudassar was another of Matty's exes. They broke up, because she thought he might be expecting her to go further – you know, *further* further, because he was older than she was. It happened a while ago, though. 'Remember he had that friend who got suspended for letting the goat out?'

'Yes! He's the friend! Um . . . *is* he the friend?'

'Yeah, the Head told him that the goat could have

been killed, because it got as far as the road and it could have caused a car crash.'

'Well, it is pretty stupid to put a goat in danger just for laughs,' I said. But Wolfie hadn't looked like such a 'bad boy'-type; I'd liked his smile, and his long swingy hair. I hated the way loads of boys at school had their hair cropped almost bald.

'OK, look, I've gotta go. But are you coming to town with me and Lee tomorrow? I'm sorry we won't be having a proper girly shop . . .' She looked at me a little apologetically, and I was actually a little hurt, but I didn't want to tell her – I didn't want her to feel bad. More often than not, now, Lee would come along to the things Matty and I had made our sort of routines. But I guiltily remembered that I'd been trying to make Matty change her plans anyway.

'Well, there's that Cadeby Wood demo thing, remember?' I said, gesturing a bit sheepishly back at one of the signs fastened to a tree.

'Oh, you're kidding,' Matty said. 'You want to spend *all* Saturday with a bunch of hippies shouting that hamburgers are more addictive than heroin, and supermarkets are the enemy of the people? What for? They're still going to build it.'

'I thought when you saw how pretty it was tonight . . . and there's your tree . . .'

'*Ex*-tree.'

'It's still a tree,' I said.

'God, no,' Matty said. 'You're nuts. I have a new CD to buy and I finally have some money, and I need a top for Georgia's birthday party.'

I looked at my fingers.

'Sorry,' Matty said, then she paused and looked at me more intensely. 'Listen, are you just put off because Lee's going? I can tell him not to come. I just said I'd help him buy a new jacket.'

'No, honestly!' I said. 'I just thought this was important.'

Matty looked relieved. 'Oh, you're nuts,' she said. 'Give us a call about it in the morning. God, it's six-thirty already, I've gotta go.'

We walked back to the road together, and Matty legged it towards her house, and I sort of lingered and looked back at the wood. I felt a bit tearful, because it was like too many things were changing all at once. Matty was bringing boys on our Saturday shopping trips, the places I'd known as a kid were being destroyed. I felt sort of scared, too, as if everything was going too fast and soon I'd have to start making big decisions about life and I wasn't ready.

But as I walked home alone, I didn't want to let my

mind go where I knew I'd start to worry myself, like thinking about GCSEs and A-levels and university and jobs and . . . stop! Instead of that, I tried to remember what I knew about Wolfie the goat boy, and whether it was because I hadn't met anyone new for a while, or maybe because trying to bring up hazy memories always feels nice, like seeing an old film you haven't seen for years, for some reason it made me smile.

Chapter 3

Matty and I had a slightly awkward phone conversation the next morning. Both of us were trying to find out if the other one was pissed off. By changing our regular routine it was almost like we were standing each other up. I thought, now we'd set the precedent, what would stop us doing it all the time, in the future?

But we both pretended we were happy about it and it was no big deal. I'd go along to the wood, 'just for a laugh', and she'd go and help Lee pick out the jacket, because boys are notoriously rubbish when it comes to knowing what suits them and I probably wouldn't be that into going round a bunch of men's departments. Besides, it'd be really good fun having different stories to share on our next girly night, to fit in around the soppy old movies. That's what we told each other.

But not-quite-falling-out with Matty had dented my confidence a bit. I changed my clothes about a thousand times before I left the house. I literally tried on every skirt I owned and settled for a little pink cord mini with long thick socks, although it didn't really feel right. When I went downstairs my mum said, 'I thought you and Matty weren't going into town today. Weren't you two going to the Wood meeting?'

I said, 'Yeah, that's right.' I didn't want to complicate things by admitting that Matty and I wouldn't be spending the day together.

She said, 'Oh, why are you dressed like that, then?'

Mums have this way of just casually saying things that completely do your head in.

'It's just a meeting,' I said. 'It's not like I'll be climbing trees or rolling around in the mud. There won't be riot police.'

'There probably *will* be police,' she said. 'You will be careful?'

'If you look out the window, you'll virtually be able to see me!' I said, although it wasn't really true.

'I'm just saying, if it gets out of hand . . .'

'Oh, come on, Mum, how can it get out of hand? Most of the people there will be as old as *you*.'

'God, surely not *that* old!' she said.

'I don't mean that.'

'Well, maybe I should come along,' she said. 'I like those trees, too. I often take some of the twigs to use in my flower arranging.'

I love my mum and always have a really good time with her, but I didn't want her to come. If there was someone there I knew, it'd look like I hadn't been allowed out without her – or worse, like I *chose* to socialise with my mother on a Saturday, or *worse* worse, *had* to socialise with my mother on a Saturday because I had no mates.

'That won't be necessary,' I said, trying to keep it casual. 'I'll bring you back the documentation and you can keep your protesting to correspondence-only. Will that do?'

'Well, I have work to catch up on,' she said, looking at a big stack of papers on the kitchen table (she was a part-time accountant, and did a lot of work at home). 'So you're safe. But I'll remind you that it's only eleven o'clock, and it's still February, so you might want to rethink the disco outfit.'

'It is not a disco outfit!' I yelled. And the thing is, I had thought it was probably a bit too much, but now I couldn't admit she was right. So I just went out in it. It was only a little pink skirt. An *old* skirt. It's not like it was a strapless dress, and I *was* wearing trainers! Though admittedly, my trainers were silver – in places.

I have found that when you hope but don't know that you're telling a lie, the thing you say has a nasty habit of coming true. So of course everyone at the Cadeby Wood protest *was* my mum's age, apart from the people who were *much older*. I was going to pretend I was just walking past and keep on walking, but then I saw the long-haired boy from the day before, Wolfie, standing with three other kids I thought I recognised from our school. I realised that I'd been hoping I'd see him again . . . There was just something about the way he looked that made me want to see more. And maybe that was why I'd taken so long deciding on an outfit – although 'outfit' is too strong a word. It was seriously just an old skirt. The other three were one boy and two girls. The boy was short and a bit tubby and trying to grow stubble, but he looked like he was funny, because the others kept laughing when he talked. The girls were both tall, with gorgeous long hair, wearing faded jeans and lovely floaty tops that were about a hundred times more elegant than my clothes, but also seemed tons more casual. My skirt felt miniscule, my long socks had started slipping down a bit, and my legs suddenly felt three times their size. Goose-pimples sprang up all over my thighs, which were blindingly white. I ducked behind a tree trunk and discreetly tried to pull the socks up again. I hoped the group wouldn't see me, but I couldn't help trying to subtly look over at them. Wolfie was leaning on another tree, nodding and smiling at something one of his friends said and, when he answered, he looked up through a straggle of hair and caught my eye for a split second. I realised I found him totally crazy-sexy. It wasn't love at first sight, because I'd been aware of him for years. It was like really seeing someone for the first time.

Then he waved me over! I looked behind me to make sure he wasn't beckoning to someone else. He laughed, and mouthed, 'Yes, you'. I pulled my skirt as far down over my thighs as it would go and scuffed a bit of soily leaf over my trainers to make them seem a bit beaten up and went over, but on the way I slightly forgot how to walk and started taking insanely big steps.

'Where's your friend today?' he said. I was used to boys asking after Matty, but my heart sank.

'She's shopping with her boyfriend,' I said. My voice sounded stupid and high. Also, I felt like a bit of a bitch, as if I was betraying Matty by trying to sabotage her with this boy because I knew I wanted him. Sure, she had a boyfriend, but still, warning him off felt a bit much.

'What's your name?' the girl with straight blond hair asked me, as if she was talking to a primary school kid. But she wasn't being bitchy. I think I just looked like I was terrified of them.

'Tessa,' I said.

'I'm Jane,' she said. 'I'm sorry Wolfie's too rude to introduce us.'

'We haven't really met,' Wolfie said.

'I thought you knew her,' Jane said. 'You said, "There's that girl who was here yesterday".'

Oh my God, I was That Girl.

'Yeah, I just *saw* her – we didn't speak.'

Well, *I* didn't speak.

'Sorry, Tessa,' Jane said. 'When he beckoned you over I assumed he knew you, and wasn't just some random bloke hassling you.'

'Hey!' Wolfie said, and grinned. 'Anyway, she came, didn't she?'

I wasn't sure what that meant.

'I'm Lara,' said the other girl, whose hair was just as fabulous, but wavy and brown. What with these girls' hair and bloody Matty's bloody perfect bob, it was like all the shampoo ads were telling the truth, and they really *had* discovered the secret to beautiful hair, but for some reason my hair refused to participate. 'He's Chunk.'

She nodded her head sideways at the other boy, who said, 'How do. Are you here to save the Wood?'

'What else is she going to be here for?' Wolfie said.

'Well, she's a bit trendy for a woodland protestor,' Chunk said.

'Shut up,' Jane said, then to me: 'He's an idiot. He thinks trendy is anyone who owns clothes made after the year 2000.' Chunk looked mock-wounded – maybe not so 'mock' – and Jane gave him a little squeeze, which made him look happy again. Like Matty, Jane seemed to have that knack of being able to relax with boys and make them relaxed. I pulled my skirt down again and tried to think of something funny or interesting to say.

'I've been coming here all my life, since before it shrank,' I said. There was enough of a silence for me to worry that I'd said something stupid.

'Yeah, me too,' Wolfie said. 'Although I don't think I've seen you here before.'

'Me neither,' I said. He held my gaze for a moment. Jane and Lara started talking amongst themselves about someone they both knew, as if they were leaving us to talk alone for a bit, and Chunk sort of closed their circle. 'I've seen foxes here,' I went on. 'I mean, even now there must still be quite a bit of wildlife.'

'When I was a kid,' Wolfie said, 'I used to believe the wood was full of wolves, because I got lost once and was chased for a bit by an Alsatian dog. I thought it was a wolf.'

'Right,' I said.

'But there aren't actually wolves,' he said, with a glint.

'Right,' I deadpanned. 'Good to know.' I couldn't believe how easily I was talking to him, kind of *playfully*.

It wasn't like we were saying anything really clever, but there was something more to it . . .

'But I liked wolves,' he said.

'Luckily,' I said.

'Oh, you mean 'cause of my name?' he said. 'Well, you're right. Chunk has a terrible fear of pineapples, and the contradiction has been the bane of his life.'

I laughed, and our eyes met.

None of us talked when the parent-like people started debating the future of the Wood, and Wolfie's gang sometimes nudged each other and made fun of the people who did talk, from time to time, but when it was finished Wolfie said to me, 'I think it was really cool that you came, anyway, especially on your own.'

'It's important,' I said, and I believed it. I hoped he believed me.

'Yeah,' he said. There was a slightly awkward pause. Wolfie's friends were ready to head off, and I was terrified that they might think they had to ask me along out of politeness and really didn't want me with them.

'OK, I've got to go,' I said. 'I'm meeting my friend, that girl who was with me yesterday. It was nice meeting you all.' I knew I sounded insanely formal and young. 'Bye, then!' And I walked away quickly, somehow forgetting how again.

chapter 4

♥

'**L**ook, help me out here,' I said. 'Did he treat you badly? I'm on *your* side . . . for the time being. Is there any reason I should not be interested in Wolfie Cole?'

The school goat just stared at me. Then it looked back at the ground and spotted an apple core, which it headed towards. I leaned over the barbed wire and stroked its back with my fingertips. Don't ask me why the school had a goat – apparently, there was a brief experimental period where gardening and farming were an alternative to housecraft in the Year Ten to Eleven syllabus, maybe because the school was quite close to the countryside, but this hadn't been an option for our year.

The goat had a little fenced-off square to live in, with a tiny open shed at the back for shelter, next to a chicken coop and some vegetable plots. Back in Year Eight, some friends of mine and I had gone through a phase of coming up here at lunch-time and feeding our sandwiches to the chickens, because for a brief, weird time eating all your sandwiches was seen as 'uncool'. We considered it hilarious to watch the chickens running around, fighting over bits of bread-crust, while we filled up on chocolate bars and crisps. From Year Ten, we were allowed outside at lunch-time, and most people went to the cafés on the main Tanner Road, and we hadn't visited the goat and chickens in ages.

Matty had taken the morning off school to go to the dentist and I was spending lunch-break alone. I'd stayed back in class to help the teacher move some books into the store cupboard and had fallen behind the main lunch-time rush. I was feeling a bit too shy to go and plonk myself with a group of friends. You know how sometimes you just don't feel up to joining in a loud conversation that's already in full swing?

'Tessa?' someone said. It was Lara, the brown wavy-haired tall girl who'd been at the Cadeby Wood meeting. She was with Jane, the sweet blonde one. 'Hi, I thought it was you,' Lara said. 'Have you started leafleting, then?'

We'd all taken some of the flyers from the meeting and been told to distribute them. I had only given them to my parents so far and asked them to take them into work. Although I'd brought some to school with the best of intentions, when it came down to it, I didn't think I could hand them out in registration or anywhere else. I was afraid of looking geeky.

'Well, a bit,' I said.

'Yeah? And what does the *goat* say about it?' Lara said. I looked at her to see if she was making fun of me or just joking and couldn't really tell.

'Oh, I think he has issues with Wolfie,' I said.

'She,' Jane said. 'But you're right – she's still in love with him. He did try to rescue her.'

'Really?' I said. 'I heard he let her run into the street.'

Lara looked a bit annoyed. 'No,' she said, and I worried I'd made a terrible mistake and she hated me now. 'What happened was, he'd asked time and time again for her to have alternative fencing or fastening. She used to have this horrible wire rope round her neck and had to walk around a little tent peg the whole time, and sometimes the wire would wind around the peg until it was about six inches long, and it was cutting into her neck, and she was actually bleeding and scabby with dried blood. But no one did anything about it. So one day Wolfie climbed over and took the wire off and let her go, just because he was so angry and, you know, worried about her. I mean, no one listens to the students, right? He thought she'd just run around the field and a teacher would have to run and catch her, and maybe someone new would see how badly she was getting hurt and do something about it. But she got a bit further than he'd expected. And she didn't run into the road. She just wandered out the back gate, where it's a closed off street, no cars . . .'

I was mortified. It was like I'd said their friend was some kind of goat killer and really he was some kind of goat hero. I waited for her to finish, then quickly said, 'God, I'm sorry, I didn't know anything about it, honestly!'

'It's OK,' Jane said, nicely. 'Why would you? It happened when we were in Year Seven or Eight, years ago – in fact you probably weren't even here. So it's kind of amazing you'd heard about it. Wolfie's going to love hearing that he's a goat-rustling legend.'

'I was just told . . .'

'Well, whatever,' Lara said. 'But Wolfie and the goat are old friends.' There was something about the way she said it that sort of sounded like she meant something deeper, like *they* were all old friends and maybe I should keep out of their business.

'We haven't really done anything about the leafleting campaign either,' Jane said, changing the subject. 'But we think we ought to do something, maybe something not part of the organised schedule, and not just get angry after it's happened. It was lovely on Saturday, standing in the trees where it was so peaceful.'

'Yeah,' I said. 'It's one of my favourite places . . .'

While I was talking, Matty came up, having got back from her dentist.

'Hi,' she said. 'Dee said she thought she saw you up here. Did I miss anything interesting this morning?' She said hi to the other two girls, who smiled.

'No, nothing,' I said. 'Matty, this is Jane and Lara. They were at the Cadeby Wood meeting on Saturday. We were just talking about it.'

'Yeah, I wanted to go,' Matty said, sounding a bit stiff. 'But I'd promised someone I'd be somewhere else.' Matty had, of course, shown no interest in the Wood the day before, but there was a softness in the way her voice trailed off, and I sensed she felt she had missed out on something. And it was true that she'd promised Lee she'd see him; maybe she'd talked down the Wood because she wanted to talk me into keeping her date with him.

'There's gonna be more, I think,' Jane said. 'You should definitely come along to the next one.'

'Yeah,' Matty said, nodding. We talked about it a bit more, but lunch was over pretty soon after, and Matty and I were going in the opposite direction to them. 'Maybe I should have gone,' Matty said to me, softly.

'I think you made the right choice. You got Lee the Diesel jacket.'

'Yeah . . . but I missed you,' she said.

'Yeah, I missed you,' I said. 'And it was pretty boring, standing around listening to like local senior citizens groups making angry speeches about the evils of progress and the modern world.'

I thought she needed to hear that it hadn't been a major social event. Even though Matty was the stylish and confident one, the one who had boys falling at her feet and always knew what to say, I sometimes found myself making fun of things I believed in or liked, to make her feel better. I wasn't sure why, maybe because I'd always sort of been the uncool one, the one we both made fun of, and it would have been wrong to change things. I didn't feel ready to make that change yet – I didn't take myself seriously as someone with my own style. And sometimes, I just felt Matty needed me to be the same, because her life was changing so much and she appreciated having someone around who she could depend on.

'But you met some people there?'

'Lara and Jane? I don't think Lara likes me. Jane's lovely, though.'

Matty nodded and smiled quite shyly. 'She's beautiful. Were there a lot of people from our school there?'

'God, no, just us. It really was full of pensioners. I got a few phone numbers from old men, actually –

they're in my purse somewhere . . .' I mimed looking for it, and Matty laughed.

'Shut up!'

'No, some of them were really quite hot. Skin not so good, sure, and some of them a bit bald, but a lot of them had brand new teeth . . .'

'Oh my God!' Matty said, and we were back on track again, laughing and relaxed. 'OK, I admit it: I'm glad I didn't go. You know I like the Wood, and I think it was a sweet idea, but it does seem kind of pointless trying to stop it. If the shop's bought the land, you're all probably just wasting your time. Sorry, but . . .'

'No, you're right,' I said. 'But it's sort of worth trying. I mean, yes, the big businesses always win, but maybe it's good that people know they're not alone in wishing it wasn't always true and that other things are important.'

'Yeah, I can see that,' Matty said. 'So there was no one else from school there?'

'A couple of guys.'

'Oh *yeah*?' Matty said. 'Why didn't you tell me this yesterday? Anyone . . . *interesting*?'

'The boy we saw in the wood the other day,' I said, keeping my voice neutral. I'd made the mistake in the past of admitting to crushes (cough JOHNCHEESEMAN cough) before I was really sure, and suddenly they were official and Matty was making them happen. I didn't want this to be taken out of my hands. And a small, immature part of me also wanted Matty's approval – her was-he-cool-enough? approval – before I went ahead and fancied him.

'Mudassar's mate?' Matty said.

'Yeah.'

'Was he with those girls?'

'Yeah.'

'You said a couple of guys?'

'Oh, someone called Chunk.'

'Yeah, I know Chunk,' Matty said. 'Hairy. Not very hot.'

'Right,' I said.

Matty didn't seem to have anything else to say, and I was going to leave it, but then she said, 'They're all a bit political, that lot, aren't they?' she said. 'Quite serious?'

'Well . . .' I said, 'They're quite funny, too.'

'Mm,' said Matty, then sighed. 'I bet the guys read newspapers . . .'

'Oh, I see what you're saying.' I laughed. 'You're talking about my quest for the perfect newspaper-reading man.'

'You're the one who's always complaining about being single!'

But I still thought Matty was only bringing it up to

make fun of me, as if she was saying, you want newspaper-readers, you get people like *that*, and the '*that*' was not what a sane person would want.

We'd all swapped e-mails at the meeting, and I updated my address book and put theirs in. I spent about an hour drafting a group e-mail to them all that said:

From: ttaylor@spectraweb.com
To: chunk@chunk-am.uk, laramcc@globernet.com,
whosjane@worldscollide.co.uk,
wolfiec@globernet.com
Subject: cadeby wood

Hi everyone

It was good meeting you all on Saturday and
great to know that other people are interested
in the future of the Wood. If there's anything
you have planned that I can be a part of, however small, please let me know.

Best,
Tessa

Really: an *hour*. I tinkered with it until the words had lost their meaning, with my mouse hovering now and again over the send button. Finally, I decided the e-mail made me look like a massive loser, and I knew the only reason I wanted to send it was to remind Wolfie he could spontaneously send me e-mails telling me I was pretty and asking me on dates. That kind of thinking was going to guarantee me disappointment. Then my brother started pestering me for the computer, and I didn't want to leave it on there for him to find and make fun of, so I deleted and trashed the mail.

'Are you sure you've finished here?' Jack asked, with unusual thoughtfulness.

'Yes,' I replied, surprised.

'Great, thanks.'

I smiled. Just before I'd left the den, he said, 'Hang on, you've got new mail.'

It was a group e-mail from Wolfie.

(!!!!!!!!!!!!!!!)

(Hm. Be cool, Tessa.)

From: wolfiec@globernet.com

To: ttaylor@spectraweb.com, chunk@chunk-am.uk,

laramcc@globernet.com,

whosjane@worldscollide.co.uk

Subject: tomorrow we fight

Guys

We will not rest till the Wood is free for
wolves and goats to roam in safety and liberty.

I nearly died. Lara and Jane had clearly *told* him what
I'd said about the goat, and, even though it was a group
e-mail, he was making fun of me. My heart was beating as
I read on.

Keep this channel free for progress reports.

Peace

Wolfie

There's only so many times you can re-read a twenty-
nine-word e-mail, but I was still at it when Jack finally
said, 'OK, OK, you said you were going?'

'Oh, sorry,' I said, and left him alone, although I
wanted to stay and keep reading the mail. It was official.
I'd fallen for the Wolf.

Chapter 5

'So he's giving it some of this and I'm like, do you even know who you're messing with? And he's like, not only do I not know, it's pretty obvious that if you *told* me who I'm messing with, I still wouldn't know, you know?' Lee said.

'God, yeah,' Matty said. (I was thinking, *Huh?*) 'So what did you say?' she asked. The three of us were hanging out after school at our favourite coffee shop, Hava Java. Matty and Lee were draped over each other in the corner, and he was stroking the top of her arm, and I was sitting a little awkwardly to one side, dividing my attention between Lee's story and a new magazine.

'So I'm like, clearly neither of us is gonna back down, but I don't want to risk a black eye before the weekend, even if I put him down for it. So I'm stood there with my hands in my pockets and I suddenly just like crack up laughing. You know, like it's really funny, 'cause it *is*, right? And I'm like, whatever man, let's forget it, it's a *lovely* T-shirt. Queen are well cool, man, and he stands there and looks at me and he's like, whatever, and then he's gone.'

'Ha! You're so cool,' Matty said. 'And I'm glad you let him off. I don't want you getting into a fight, even with a Queen fan.' She held his chin in one hand and kissed his cheek.

'It's hardly a fair fight,' Lee said, downing his cup of tea modestly.

Lee could be nice and funny and he was definitely cool and trendy, and Matty had told me enough things about how amazing he was when they were alone – how he flattered her and bought her things; but just *occasionally*, I couldn't stand him. I knew this was something to do with being jealous of the fact that Lee had 'stolen' my best friend and got to spend so much time with her. And I knew it had something to do with me being jealous of *Matty*, because she had someone special, a boy she could talk about who stroked her arm in public, and it was proof that she was prettier and sexier and more mature than me. I knew all this and felt crap about it. But pushing that to one side for an *instant*, Lee could really be a boring, self-important prick.

I worried that Matty couldn't see this about him. I also worried that Matty *could* see this about him and was embarrassed about me seeing it. I didn't want her to be: I didn't want her to have another reason to see less of me, and I definitely didn't want her to think I judged her boyfriend (although I did) or thought less of her because of him (because that wasn't true at all).

I probably spent too much time worrying about me and Lee and Matty.

But I needed a break, and said I was going to the counter to get another drink and did they want anything. Lee wanted another milky, sugary tea; Matty, her usual, skimmed milk latte (a Matty-latty). I figured I'd go for a strong espresso, to keep me awake through Lee's next story. I was standing, drumming my fingers on the counter, staring into space, when the bloke behind me in the queue nudged my upper arm with his, but I wasn't expecting it, got unbalanced and started falling. He grabbed my forearm to keep me upright.

'Whoops, sorry,' he said with a laugh. 'I didn't mean to bump you so hard.' I nearly gasped with delight – it was Wolfie. When he'd pulled me up straight again, he let go of my arm. 'I'm glad I found you – I've got some exciting news.'

Had he been looking for me? 'Oh wow, about Cadeby Wood?' I asked.

'Yeah, oh, your coffees are ready.' He nodded towards the end of the counter, where the assistant was putting the cups.

'Well . . .' I wanted to let him know I was too

interested in his news to think about coffee, but I was a bit worried about taking Lee and Matty stone cold drinks, and this was probably the best time for a break. 'Hang on, I'll be right back.'

I took Lee's tea and Matty's latte to them and slid them across the table. 'I won't be long,' I said. 'I've just got . . .'

'Is that tramp bothering you?' Lee said, and laughed.

'Um . . .' I said.

'Shhh,' Matty said. She looked embarrassed and shrugged at me.

I quickly shook my head at her, letting her know it was OK. 'I won't be long,' I said.

I went back to Wolfie, who was waiting with my espresso.

'A quid twenty for a quarter of an egg cup of coffee,' he said. 'You're so decadent.'

'It's not the size, it's the strength,' I said. I knew while I was saying it that he might read it as a sort of cool innuendo, because I'm not very tall, but I hoped it wasn't too flirty.

He smiled and raised one eyebrow. 'I bet. So listen, Chunk's dad is Features Editor for the local paper, and he's managed to get us – *us* – this is insane, a whole page. It's nominally for our school, like a "schoolkids talk" feature; but, like, sod the rest of the school – they weren't there, and Chunk says this *is* ours anyway. We're going to put together a presentation. Lara's a brilliant writer . . .'

I drooped a little bit, thinking maybe he was in love with Lara.

'. . . Chunk's also great, really funny, but sarcastic and Jane's really smart. It's going to be great.'

'And . . . ?' It occurred to me that there wasn't really anything for me to do. I sipped my espresso. Actually I didn't like espresso – *yet* – but I'd made a new year's resolution to develop a taste for it, because I thought it was more sophisticated than my usual hot chocolate with squirty cream. I usually had to put tons of sugar in it, but was pretending to Wolfie that I drank it straight.

'Oh we totally want you to help. You're very sincere and . . . you know, *passionate* when you talk about the wood (I felt myself blush when he used the word 'passionate'). I bet you'll come up with something good. I'm taking some pictures. We're going to make it look really professional – take it seriously. Tug at some heartstrings and get some serious backing. The store still has to get through another council appeal for planning permission before they can start, and you never know.'

'God, do you really think we could make a difference?'

'It's got to be worth a try,' he said. 'Listen, how about if you come with me now and we can scope out some shots for me to take that would work with the thing you're gonna write. But I know it's a bit of a cheek, you're with your friends . . .' He glanced at me, looking almost shy, utterly gorgeous, then looked down. 'We could do it another time, if you're too busy. It's OK.'

'No, I mean, there must be a deadline, right?' I said, hopefully.

'Oh yeah, there's a deadline of *course* – the sooner the better.'

'I think Matty and Lee'll be fine without me,' I said, nodding. 'I'll just go and tell them I have to go.'

'Wait!' Wolfie said, urgently.

'What?'

'But you've still got all that coffee to drink.'

I looked at him, having taken at least three whole seconds to realise he was joking, and then I just let out this huge laugh.

'I'll be right back,' I said again.

'I'll be here,' he said, glancing over at Lee and Matty.

'Is everything OK?' Matty said, narrowing her eyes while she tried to work me out, and why I'd left them for so long.

'Yeah, it's good,' I said breezily. 'Wolfie and his mates are doing a sort of feature for the local paper, about the Wood, you know, and the protest, and I said I'd give them a hand. There's just a bit of a rush, because the paper's given them a deadline and they have to organise it, and we just want to talk about it for a bit. And you know how much homework we've got tonight.'

'Yeah, sure,' Matty said. 'I just wanted to know everything was OK . . .'

'So what's with the crusty-love?' Lee said. 'You sure you want to hang out with those weirdos? You'll come back with your nose pierced and your hair in dreadlocks.'

'It's just about this wood . . .' I said.

'I told him,' Matty said.

'Smoking da gan-jaaaa,' Lee said. 'Da ganja weeeed.'

'They're not crusties,' I said. I wondered if I should stay until I could assure Matty I really *wanted* to go with Wolfie and wasn't just worried about cramping her style. But this was not a good time to admit I had a crush on him.

'E me, message me,' Matty said.

'*Sure,*' I said. 'I'll be home before you.'

The sun was low and shining a deep gold when we got to the Wood. Wolfie's face was striped with shadows and, when the sun broke through the branches with dazzling rays, he looked beautiful – straight swingy hair catching the low light, his eyes narrowed against the glare. It wasn't cold, but I found myself trembling all over, shivering sometimes, and hoped he didn't see. I was talking too much, saying things that weren't worth saying. He was much quieter, but when he did talk he was funny, or lovely. He talked about how much he loved the peacefulness, and at that point I told myself, *Shut up, Tessa – wait until he speaks.* Enjoy *the silence*! I was sure I was annoying him by now.

'Sorry, I'm talking too much,' I said.

'No. You're not,' he said. 'The point of this was for me to get a feel of how you think of the Wood – what you're going to say. And then I'll come back tomorrow and get down to it.'

'I suppose I haven't really had a chance to think it through yet. I could write something tonight and come back with you?' I said, and then closed my eyes and waited for the rejection. This was, in Tessa World, a very big and very obvious pass. He didn't answer for too long. I opened my eyes. He was looking straight at me. Just say it, I thought, just say no. Just say you need to be alone to work properly, but please let me down gently.

'I'd love that,' he said. This time I think I might actually have gasped.

Neither of us spoke and we just looked at each other, and he frowned just slightly, and I let my lips part just slightly, and I was thinking, please come here and kiss me, just kiss me, just once – that would be enough to make me happy for, oh, for ever, and I held my breath.

Then he said, 'OK, shall we meet here tomorrow after school? As early as possible, because we want to get good light, I mean, even though this is nice now it won't look as good in a black and white . . .' and he started walking back out of the wood away from me. I followed, running to keep up.

I *did* get home before Matty.

Chapter 6

When I woke up I had about five seconds of normality and then I remembered the previous evening and what a fool I'd made of myself. I pulled the sheets over my head and groaned, wondering if I could get away with not getting up at all. Better make it early, Wolfie had said, and no wonder, when all it took was a bit of sunset to make me gape at him like a lost puppy. He must have known what was on my mind. How could I have thought he'd want to kiss me? For one thing, he was probably on the verge of going out with Lara – what with the way she defended him, the way he talked about her in that admiring way, and the fact that she had that gorgeous hair – and if he told his mates that I had some stupid crush on him, I'd never be able to face any of them again.

Then there was Matty, who was apologetic and worried about making me feel left out, and she had no idea that I'd been trying to get away so I could keep my crush a secret from her. I was being a terrible friend. But I didn't want to tell her at all, now that I knew Wolfie wasn't ever going to feel the same way about me. I was fed up with only confiding my romantic failings to her.

It was a busy day at school and we only really caught up with each other at the end of it in a free period.

'So, yesterday,' Matty said, 'I think Lee said a lot of stupid stuff, and I want you to know it's not what I think, and it's not what *he* thinks, even. It's just his sense of humour is sometimes a bit dodgy.'

'Honestly, it's fine,' I said.

'I do *not* want you and me to grow apart because you think my boyfriend doesn't know when to stop.'

'Oh, Matty, don't be nuts. You know you can't get rid of me. Why would the things he said upset me, anyway?'

'Because you're totally into Wolfie Cole,' Matty said.

I gaped at her.

'I'm right, aren't I?' she said.

I gaped at her some more.

She smiled. 'I *am* right, then. Good, I'm glad I can still see right through you. Oh, you can so get him – this is going to be great. When are you seeing him next?'

'Well, this evening, I'm supposed to be going to . . . Oh, but listen, Matt, forget it anyway, because I've already made it obvious and he's not interested. So yes, I fancy Wolfie, and yes, you're some kind of evil genius, but it's no good, and let's not get upset about it – there's plenty more fish in the sea.'

'What are you talking about? What happened?' Matty said.

I told her about the day before, in the Wood: how I'd stood right next to him, how I'd stared up at him with my lips open and then closed my eyes – all the techniques Matty herself had taught me to use to show a boy I was interested. And he'd legged it out of the wood like it was full of angry bears, and moved up the time of our next meeting to make it before tea, nowhere near date-time, so I wouldn't get the wrong idea.

'But you don't *know* this for sure,' Matty said.

'He had every chance to let me know he felt the same way as me, and he couldn't get away fast enough,' I said.

'Well,' Matty said. 'You've still got tonight to change his mind. What are you wearing?'

'This,' I said. 'We're going straight after school.'

Matty looked at me. I was wearing my oldest jeans and no make-up, and my hair was scraped back in a ponytail. I also had a *fabulous* new spot on my chin.

'You've got time to change,' she said.

'But nothing to change into. Anyway, don't you see? I wore this on purpose. Now he knows I fancy him, I have to look the *opposite* of trying to get him. If I turned up in a little skirt and make-up, he'd just call the whole thing off in horror.'

'Or,' Matty said, taking my hair out of its stubby little ponytail, 'now, he'll think you've hippie-fied yourself a bit to try to be the kind of girl he'd go for. Dressing down, becoming less *materialistic* . . .'

'Nooooo!' I said. 'Oh my God, there's no way he could think that. Is there? No, I bet he thinks I'm too shallow to even be able to empathise enough to imagine that there was a possibility that . . .'

'Shut up! You're doing my head in,' Matty said. 'Have you seen him yet today?'

'No. But what diff–'

'Come on,' she said. 'There's no time to lose.'

Matty took me to the drama studio, where there were little changing rooms to the side, and sat me down.

'OK, have you got a T-shirt under there?' she said, looking at my baggy jumper.

'Yes, but it's cold.'

'Doesn't matter – you're taking my denim jacket. Is it a pretty one? Come on, get that thing off.'

It was a black T-shirt with a cute little drawing of a flower with a face on it, in white.

'Good,' Matty said. 'All is not lost. Now, do you have your make-up with you?'

'You know I only wear mascara,' I said.

'I know, I know,' Matty said. 'And you're bloody well not today, even. Luckily, I am always fully armed . . .'

She sat me down and for the next ten minutes smudged, powdered and painted my face. Part of me was terrified, I was thinking, 'Oh my God, she's going to make me look like a complete tart,' but I was also secretly pleased, because I'd always wanted a 'but Miss Taylor, you're beautiful' moment. Basically, though, I knew I was just one of those girls who looked terrible in lots of make-up and I didn't fancy her chances.

'Here,' she said, handing me her compact mirror. I looked. I looked again. It looked as if I wasn't wearing any make-up. I looked like me, but so much better. And my new friend, Spotty McZit, appeared to have gone *completely*.

'What did you . . . ?' I said.

I touched it, to feel where it was, and Matty screamed. 'Agh! No touchy! Now off you go to the ball.'

'Matty . . .' I said, feeling all sentimental.

'Yeah, I know,' Matty said.

But my confidence started to drain away when I was on my own again. I cringed when I remembered the way I'd opened my eyes to find him just looking at me, clearly embarrassed, and the way he'd suggested we met earlier rather than later, because he obviously thought it was too late to pull out altogether. I decided I would just stick it out, be a grown-up about it. I wouldn't talk too much like I had the day before, or stare at him like a lovesick idiot, and, when it was done, I was going to be the first one to say that I had to go, and not leave it dangling until he had to come up with excuses to get rid of me.

Wolfie was leaning on the gate where we said we'd meet – alone, staring at the sky, not looking out for me. I thought that he must have been hoping I wouldn't turn up. He was wearing faded cords and a fitted black shirt. I ignored the way my heart was pumping blood recklessly round my body, pulled myself together and called his name.

I'd been terrified I'd run out of things to say to him on the way there, but it was easy. I started off talking about the Wood, and the notes I'd started to write, hoping he wouldn't ask me to show him any of them, because they were all scrawled in a girly pink notebook. Then he asked me questions and it took the pressure off me, and suddenly we were just talking without thinking, and, not only was I not worried about silences, I was waiting for Wolfie to finish talking so I wouldn't interrupt him constantly, and he was funny and laughing, and enthusiastic and interested.

He really seemed to get me, and I didn't feel I had to explain anything, and I just couldn't believe we'd got over yesterday's embarrassment so smoothly. I was talking about the things I could remember of spending time in the woods as a kid: Matty and me looking for foxes because we'd just read a book called *Little Red Fox* and loved it, my mum personalising fairy tales like *Snow White* as we walked through the kind of scenery that was in the stories. My brother and I collecting conkers, both of us climbing trees and trying to rig up secret hide-outs in their branches, and then we were there, suddenly already in the wood, and Wolfie had whipped out his camera and was looking through the lens.

As he concentrated, I suddenly realised I'd broken my don't-talk-too-much rule, but I'd felt so relaxed, I was sure that it was allowed. Still, I made up my mind to ease off a bit. In the silence, I started wondering if Wolfie had really been interested in all the childish crap I'd just come out with. He was a little way from me, and I didn't want to look as though I was following him or staring at him, so I walked slowly around, trying to remember the names of flowers my mum had taught me. Then the next time I looked up, he was pointing his camera at me. I cried out in protest and put my hands in front of my face.

'What's wrong?' he said, softly, as if he really couldn't understand.

'I look horrible in photographs. And I look horrible today. So that's like horrible squared.'

He walked a few paces closer.

'You look great. But if you don't like being photographed, that's OK. Lots of people don't. Lara, for instance, is incredibly photogenic, but she's camera-shy.'

I got the message. Lara is beautiful: don't waste your time, kid.

'So did the wolf catch you?' I said.

He looked confused for a moment. 'Ah, the Alsatian?' he said.

'Well, don't spoil the ending,' I said.

He laughed. 'Well, the wolf saw me; I saw the wolf, and it started running after me, barking.'

'My God! Don't wolves howl?'

'I believe wolves make a *variety* of noises, and some of them can sound like a common dog bark.'

'I *see* . . .'

'I knew you would. So I'm running away as fast as I can in my shorts and wellies . . .'

I smiled very widely at the image.

'. . . the wolf's in hot pursuit. I'm terrified – did I

mention the fact that it didn't have an owner with it? It was just a loose dog.'

'Big dogs are just as dangerous as wolves anyway,' I said.

He smiled. 'That's a *very* good point. It adds a real sense of menace to the story, too. So I'm running, and the wolf is running, and the toe of my wellie gets trapped under a raised tree root – it comes right off my foot, but I'm so scared I don't stop. Then my socked foot lands on a sharp rock – the pain is . . . *intense* . . . and I fall over, and the wolf catches up, stands over me, bares its big teeth and then . . .'

'And then?'

'It licks me all over my face.'

I giggled, and he lifted his camera and took a picture.

'Not fair!' I protested.

'You looked pretty,' he said. Then, looking away from me, he added, 'We probably need byline pictures of all our contributors.'

He's worried I'm getting ideas again, I thought. We were both quiet for a moment.

'Show me your friend Matty's tree,' he said.

I took him to the James Lvs Matilda tree and he traced their names with his finger.

'Wanton vandalism of nature's beautiful design,' he said, and I looked at him in disbelief, and then realised he was joking.

'It lasted longer than their love affair,' I said, and thought to myself, but not longer than James's love, because that was strangely comforting.

'Yeah, she's going out with that . . . well, it doesn't matter,' Wolfie said.

'I get the feeling you don't get on with Lee,' I said. They were in the same year, so I guessed they knew each other. I couldn't believe I was talking to Wolfie in this relaxed, unguarded way.

'He's your friend's boyfriend,' Wolfie said. 'It wouldn't be very sensible for me to talk about him.'

'I'm not going to *tell* him,' I said.

'I mean, because you'll think less of me,' he said.

'But that's not true!' I said. 'I'm not Lee's number one fan myself.'

'Even so . . .' he said.

'Well, you're right. I shouldn't bitch about my best friend's boyfriend to someone I hardly know.'

'Well, I'd like to think you think you know me a bit now,' Wolfie said. 'This is very nearly a date.' I didn't let myself believe he meant it.

'Except you don't fancy me,' I said, sounding exactly as I'd promised myself I wouldn't.

'Is that right?' Wolfie said.

'Well, obviously,' I said. 'I mean, you fancy Lara, right?'

'Do I?'

'And even if you didn't, why . . .' His face was now close to mine and I had to stop talking because I was confused and nervous. 'But yesterday . . .'

'Yesterday I had more self-control,' he said, 'and I didn't want you to think I was, you know, like, "Come into the woods with me, I'll show you some . . . *wildlife*". I'm serious about this article, and it's not about trying to . . . and I didn't know how you felt . . . but today I've listened to you telling stories that make you even sweeter, and look at you through a lens that shows me how beautiful you are, and I'm losing the fight.' I leaned back against Matty's tree, my hands tucked behind me, and Wolfie rested his arm on the trunk above me. 'Am I . . . if I'm barking up the wrong tree . . .' and we both held our breath hoping the bad pun wouldn't break the spell, '. . . you have to let me know now.'

'You're not,' I whispered. He kissed me. His lips were so soft, I felt dizzy, and when I opened my eyes, he was still there.

'I'm sorry,' he said.

'Why?' I said.

'You must think I'm a creep. Tessa, I swear I didn't plan this. I didn't bring you here to make a move.'

'Shhh,' I said, and kissed him back.

chapter 7

My dad had changed out of his suit into the Simpsons T-shirt I'd bought him for his birthday, and was coming downstairs at the moment Matty came in.

'Matilda,' he said. 'If I'd been told you were coming round I'd have worn something more fashionable.' My dad loved Matty because she talked to him like they were both adults. Everyone else our age was monosyllabic and shy with parents, and I was no exception, but Matty was always Matty – no one rattled her.

'Fashion fades, Bob. Style never does,' Matty said. I knew that I would never be old enough to talk like Matty.

'It takes someone with style to know that,' Dad said. 'Are you here to steal my broadband?'

'I am here,' Matty said haughtily, 'to do coursework with Tessa.'

'Course you are,' Dad said. 'Let us know if you need coffee, tea, food, hard liquor . . .'

'The forty Bensons I've got in my bag should keep us going, thanks,' Matty said.

'Good,' Dad said. 'I'll leave you to it.'

'Has he e-mailed yet?' Matty said, when the door to the den was closed.

'He e-mailed as soon as he got in yesterday, but I only saw it today when I got in.'

'Show me?'

I found the e-mail.

From: wolfiec@globernet.com

To: ttaylor@spectraweb.com

Subject: . . .

Tessa

Wow. I'd love to see you again and have it not be about saving trees. Not that saving trees isn't very important. Oh yeah. Gotta save those trees. Which reminds me, I was supposed to tell you we're all going back to Chunk's on Friday to put our pitch together. Really hope you can make it. Really hope you and I can get some time to talk afterwards.

W

'What do you think?' I said to Matty, chewing my bottom lip.

'Yeah . . .' she said, but she didn't sound sure. 'It's cute.'

'What's wrong with it?' I said.

'Nothing,' she said.

'Except . . . ?'

'He's a bit . . . well, nothing,' Matty said.

'You can't do that,' I said. 'What?'

'He's just a bit . . .' she trailed off.

'Oh come on, Matty, you're driving me mad.'

'He's a bit serious? "Gotta save those trees"?'

'He's *joking*,' I said. 'He said he didn't want me to think he was just taking me into the woods to try to snog me, so he's pretending he has to remember to pretend the Wood is important.'

'Wow, you get all that just from the e-mail, do you?' Matty said, dubiously.

I threw my hands up in disbelief. Of course I got it just from the e-mail: I *knew* him now – I really *got* him.

Then I thought, oh God, I hardly know him – what if she's right? Then I thought, well what if she *is* right: he wants to save the Wood – what's wrong with that? But it would mean that Matty was right about him being a bit serious.

But was there anything wrong with someone who was a bit serious, when I was always moaning on about boys being too shallow? God, someone take me out of my head for five minutes!

'And it's not that *romantic*, is it?' Matty said. 'I mean, it's nice enough, but . . .'

'But *he* is,' I said. 'When he was kissing me, he said the loveliest things.'

'They *all* do that when you're *kissing* them,' Matty said. 'To keep you kissing them.'

'God, what's *wrong* with you?' I said, actually beginning to lose my temper. 'I have been single my entire life and when I finally show some interest in someone, you're acting like I should forget about it!'

'That's *why*!' Matty said. 'You know I've wasted too much time on losers, and I want to make sure this guy's the real deal before my best friend goes and falls for him. You've watched me get my heart broken enough, haven't you? I'm just looking out for you.'

Well, Matty hadn't really had her heart broken all that much. She'd cried a bit after boys she'd just finished with had said really nasty things to her or about her, and she'd cried a bit after boys she'd finished with had found new girlfriends, sometimes, but there hadn't been much heartbreak or dumping-of-Matty in Matty's life.

'Yeah, I know,' I said. 'And I love you for it. I'm just nervous. And excited. And scared. And so so so so happy!'

'Good,' Matty said. 'It's time someone as gorgeous as you had a shot of proper romance.'

'And scared . . .' I whined.

'I know. Don't worry, we'll proceed with caution. Have you already replied?'

Jack knocked on the door and asked if we were done with the computer because he wanted to play 'Ramraider 3' on it. Then I heard my mum shout, 'Leave them alone, Jack. They're working.'

We weren't working, of course, but e-mails from boys rank above 'Ramraider 3'. We waited a couple of seconds, until there was silence from Jack.

'OK, yes, I sent back a reply,' I told Matty.

'The same night?' Matty said.

'No, when I got in today,' I said. 'I only just saw it, remember?'

'That's good: you sent him to bed worrying that he'd done the wrong thing and maybe frightened you away.'

'But, Matt, I'm no good at playing games. I just really like him.'

'Has he texted you?'

'He doesn't have a mobile.'

62

'Why on earth not?' Matty said.

'He's . . . oh, he's anti-mobile phones. He says there's too much emphasis on everyone being constantly available and in touch in the modern world, and everyone's getting brain tumours, kidding themselves that they're more important than they actually are.'

'Oh,' Matty said. 'He's a real cheery bunny. He must be an amazing kisser.'

'I . . .' I paused. I wasn't much of an expert. I'd been a bit worried that my own technique was lacking, to be honest.

'Well is he?' Matty said. 'On a scale of John Cheeseman to how you think Tobey Maguire kisses?'

'Spider-Man! Not Cheese-Man!'

'It's OK if he isn't perfect. It's one of the things you can change about them, as long as he shows some initial promise.'

'Matty, my knees went weak. My head started spinning . . .'

'Are you sure he didn't spike your Tizer with gin?'

'Stop it, you! There was no Tizer, no gin, just a perrrrfect kiss.'

'I remember my first kiss with Lee,' Matty said. 'He was still a smoker at the time, and his mouth tasted all bitter . . .'

'Eurgh,' I said. 'Why would you want to snog him again?'

'Because even with the fags, it was . . . oh . . . just so nice. And I knew I'd be able to stop him smoking, and I did – making them give up fags is one of the ways you can change them.'

'All right,' I said. 'But I don't want to change anything about Wolfie.'

Matty smiled at me as if she knew something I didn't.

'I'm not going to change my mind!' I said.

'I didn't say anything,' she said.

We read my reply to his e-mail, and Matty said it was OK – I hadn't given too much away. But Matty thought it was important to play hard to get and I didn't see any point in *me* doing that when a) I was not hard to get, and b) I didn't want there to be *any* reason Wolfie might change his mind about me. Matty said I didn't understand – the only way of testing whether boys were worth it was making them do a bit of work to get you, and that way you avoided getting hurt. I wanted to tell her that I could just *tell* Wolfie was a nice guy, and that he might not fancy me enough, or he might stop fancying me, but I couldn't imagine him ever treating anyone badly. I knew Matty would just say I didn't know as much about boys as her.

'Look, I don't know what's going to happen,' I said. 'It's all too early. I should shut up.'

'This is the first boy you've been really interested in in ages,' Matty said softly. 'And you've snogged him. I think it's not so bad to mention it . . . after all, you tried to keep fancying him a secret from me.'

'I did not!'

'Well, how come I had to ask you about him?' Matty said.

I blushed. 'Well . . . I just didn't want to make a fool of myself.'

'Are you sure it wasn't because Lee . . . said stuff about him?'

'No. I mean, yes, I'm sure.'

'Lee's just different, you know? They're really different people.'

'Yeah, I know,' I said. 'And Wolfie *is* a bit scruffy. It's not like he said anything mean.'

'The scruffy thing? You'll be able to change that,' Matty said, with a sly smile.

'I don't want to!' I said, and we both started giggling.

I thought Matty was almost trying too hard to tell me that when it came to boyfriends, she'd seen it, done it, and bought the soundtrack. I was scared it was because

I'd been so one-track all day. I hadn't had a chance to see Wolfie around, because Matty and I had spent all of lunch-break helping the librarian sort through returned books in her stock cupboard. I'd spent the whole time talking about me and Wolfie, and I was afraid that either it sounded like boasting, or that Matty might think I hadn't known him long enough to be so sure he really liked me. It was hard to find the right balance. Matty was the one who had new romances and I was the one who got excited for her and made jokes about being perpetually single; this way around it was all new territory. But, if we both had boyfriends who didn't like each other, would we never be able to spend time together as couples? Worse, what if he and Matty didn't get on? The idea that the thing I wanted most might cause as many problems as it solved was worrying. Bigger than all of this, though, was the fact that Wolfie hadn't actually properly asked me out, and I would have about a thousand chances over the next week to put him off me. Maybe I already had, by not replying to his e-mail until nearly twenty-four hours later. Despite what I'd told Matty about not playing hard to get, it was possible that I'd accidentally played it too well.

chapter 8

Wolfie obviously hadn't said anything to his friends about me and us. We went round to Chunk's after school, and Chunk's mum was quite posh and frosty, and I tried not to stare at Wolfie, and tried not to talk too much. I read them my little article about what the Wood meant to me. They *made* me read it out loud, and I could feel my neck getting hot, and my cheeks going red, and my voice cracked a little. When I'd finished, I thought they were all going to burst out laughing. They didn't, but I did think I'd die of embarrassment.

'It's so sweet,' Jane said. 'That's going to pull at all the grannies' heartstrings.' I knew she was being nice, but I realised she must have thought that it was quite babyish. Lara's contribution was incisive and highly political and just incredibly clever – so much that I nearly laughed out loud at the difference between hers and mine. Wolfie laid out his pictures, modestly talking us through them, and they were wonderful. The woods looked deep and over-grown and magical, with no hint of the way they'd been whittled down over the years to allow for more housing. Even if nothing happened between us, I thought briefly, I would be happy if I just got to keep one of those pictures – but I didn't dare ask him for one. And I was so *relieved* that he hadn't included the photo he'd taken of me when we were there.

Chunk's newspaper-man dad came in and asked us a few questions, and I certainly didn't respond to them the way Matty does with my dad. I just sat weirdly on the arm of the sofa, because there weren't enough places to sit, and squeaked when I was spoken to, and all the time I was thinking, whatever Wolfie thought of me before, now he must think I'm an absolute *idiot*, and there's no way he's going to want some time to talk alone after this.

Chunk's dad leafed through Wolfie's photos, took one of the plainer, larger views out and said, 'I suppose this'll be the one for us . . . although I'm afraid we might have to send round one of our guys anyway. You know, there are standard types of image we use – we're not the Photographers' Gallery,' and laughed.

Wolfie said, 'Sure, I knew that might happen.' His face was blank, and Chunk's dad was sort of complimenting his picture, but I guessed he must be hurt.

When Jane and Lara said they had to get home for tea, and Chunk said he had work to do, I glanced at

Wolfie and said I'd be getting along too, but he brushed past me and whispered, 'Don't run off.'

When we were alone in the street he took my hand.

'Are you wondering why I didn't tell anyone . . . or are you glad I didn't?' he said. His brown eyes met mine.

'Er . . .' I said, not knowing the right answer. I went for the truth. 'I suppose I was wondering if you'd changed your mind,' I said.

He smiled and kissed me gently. '*I* haven't.'

'Well . . .'

'I wasn't sure about you,' he said. 'And it's best not to tell your friends what you're up to in your love life, don't you find?' I agreed, even though I didn't have very much to go on. 'Are your parents expecting you back soon, or can I make you something to eat?'

Too much happening all at once! Bloody hell, was he going to take me back to his place? Was I going to meet his parents? Was he just going to throw me on his bed and ravish me? Would saying yes to something to eat mean acceptance of any or all of these possibilities?

'Just something simple,' Wolfie said. 'But I have to warn you, it's going to be veggie . . .'

I still didn't say anything, and was wondering if I'd lost the ability to speak.

'Just, you know, *food*,' Wolfie said, frowning with

mock-confusion. 'You don't have to agree to marry me if it's good.'

I laughed with relief. Relief that he wasn't running away while he still had the chance from the crazy, indecisive girl.

'But,' he said, 'if it's *very* good, you might want to consider sleeping with me. I'm KIDDING!'

There wasn't time for my face to register any surprise, so I was sure he *was* kidding, and I just told myself to grow up. This was what happened when you reached the age of sixteen without having had a boyfriend. You acted like a nutcase when any boy talked to you. I should have paid more attention to Matty – only she'd probably have advised something like going straight home and not calling for a week . . . and I was hungry.

'OK, I told my mum I'd text if I was going to stay out, so I'll text her. And food would be great.'

'Well, don't expect too much,' Wolfie said. 'I'm not the world's best cook. I just sort of . . . fling things together.'

I nodded. 'I like . . .' (oh no! Don't say 'flings'!) '. . . flung things,' I said, and he laughed.

As we walked to his place together, I was getting visions of a bohemian hippie pad with tie-dyed rugs on the walls and patchouli incense smoking in every corner, and his mum running around barefoot with long hair and finger-cymbals – but not cooking because it was demeaning to have rigid gender roles – and his dad playing the sitar in the corner.

But it was a completely ordinary house. It was very small and also pretty messy. There was an empty pizza box on the crumb-covered kitchen counter, and the sink was full of unwashed dishes and a pan with dried-out scrambled egg. No one else was home.

'Ah. You're probably looking at the mess,' Wolfie said. 'You're probably thinking, "Who is this slob and what am I doing here?"'

'It's just a few dishes,' I said.

'No, it's messy,' he said. 'I'm sorry – I should have thought this through better. My dad must have left it like this. He sometimes only starts work after lunch.'

'Really, it doesn't offend me,' I said. His sudden unexpected anxiousness was making me smile, and making me more confident. 'What time will he be in?'

'I don't know,' Wolfie said. 'He's a computer rep and he has to drive quite a long way away most days, so he's sometimes out quite late in the evening. He probably won't be back until after you've gone.' I did worry for a moment about the wisdom of going into an empty house with a boy I hadn't known very long, but I felt very safe with him.

'Let me wash up,' I said. 'You get the food.'

'No, I can't invite you round and have you *clean* for me.'

'You're making me dinner,' I said. 'It's a good deal.'

I started filling the sink with soapy water, but I couldn't help peeking when he went to the fridge. It was stacked high with prick and heat ready-meals, a couple of bottles of beer, custard tarts – all except for one shelf, which was full of brown paper bags of mushrooms, fresh tomatoes, apples, celery sticks, carrots with long green stems, organic milk and butter. He caught me looking.

'Yeah, don't worry. My dad and I have very different styles of cuisine.'

'Don't you eat together?' I said.

'Are you kidding? My dad doesn't like to eat anything that didn't have parents.'

'Oh.'

'You eat meat, I take it.'

'Yeah. Do you hate me?'

'Of course not. I suppose I'm surprised. You seem to love the wildlife in the Wood so much; you're self-aware and green and . . .' He shrugged. 'None of my business . . . if you want to eat Bambi and Thumper.' He was grinning when he said it, so I didn't feel too bad.

'OK, first of all, I just never really thought about it, and my parents do most of the cooking – I'm not . . . *Jamie Oliver*, like you obviously are, and I just eat whatever they give me. Second, I don't eat rabbits and deer. I'm not . . . .'

'What else are you not?' he said, and reached out to touch my cheek, smiling.

'I'm not Henry the Eighth,' I said, smiling, too. Wolfie leaned towards me and kissed me.

'I hope not,' he said. 'I don't like kissing people with beards. It's scratchy.'

'So . . . I'm not . . . mmm.' I couldn't think straight when he was kissing me. 'Where was I?'

'You weren't being Henry the Eighth.'

'Right. So I eat the odd chicken, but chickens don't have nice lives. I'm putting them out of their misery, and pigs? Pigs wouldn't *exist* if I didn't eat them. There are no wild pigs, you know.'

'I see. So you and your . . . *kind* are doing the pigs a favour by granting them life so you can eat them.'

'Well . . . yeah, I suppose we are.'

'Really, you care more about animals than I do,' he said softly, still kissing me.

'I'm glad you see things my way,' I whispered.

'But we're eating tempeh tonight,' Wolfie said.

73

'Can't wait,' I said.

Yeah, I didn't know what tempeh was either, but his stir fry was delicious. It got dark outside, but I was finding it hard to tear myself away. He didn't take me to his bedroom – maybe that was messy, too. We just stayed at the kitchen table, chatting and laughing.

'So where does the name Wolfie come from?' I asked him. 'Is it short for Wolfgang?'

'Actually, like all the best things, it started in Cadeby Wood,' he said.

'No, is that true? Not because you got chased by a dog!'

'I'm afraid so. I still thought it was a wolf when I got home and told my dad about it, and he showed me a picture of a wolf, and I was like, "Yeah, yeah, it was like that, but darker". It was only later, when we saw an Alsatian together, and I pointed it out as a wolf, that I found out. So until then, I thought I had calmed the savage beast and that I had an affinity for them, and I started reading books like *White Fang* and *Call of the Wild*, and collecting stuff on wolves – I was really young, remember – and my dad called me Wolfie, so my mates did too. And it stuck.'

'What's your real name?'

'David.'

'It's a nice name,' I said.

'Would you rather call me David?' he asked.

'Would you let me?'

'I'm crazy about you,' Wolfie said.

'You look more like a Wolfie,' I said.

When we got to my gate, he held my hands in his and looked at me with his head tilted.

'Tomorrow?' he said.

'I can't,' I said. He nodded. 'I have a thing with Matty; I wish I could . . .'

He kissed my forehead very lightly. 'See Matty. I'm happy to wait.'

My house was warm and noisy as I closed the door behind me. My mum was writing letters at the kitchen table with a classical music CD playing in the background and my dad was watching a movie with my brother. I said hi to my mum – she smiled: she looked beautiful that evening – then I went straight up to my bedroom. I flopped on to my bed and hugged my shoulders and laughed, still finding it hard to believe this kind of thing could happen to me.

Chapter 9

So I became quite famous at school for a couple of weeks. First, for the Cadeby Wood piece, which some people laughed at me for, what with the references to fairies and stuff. Matty wasn't best pleased, because she'd been dragged into it – I'd mentioned her in my article. She said it wasn't good for her image, or mine. The second reason I was famous was because Wolfie and I were an item, and my friends were amazed.

'He is good-looking,' Becca said, 'under all that long hair. I can see what you see in him. I like a more clean-cut type of boy, though. Can't you make him cut it?'

'I love his hair,' I said.

'Does he smoke like tons of dope?' Charlotte asked.

'Nope,' I said.

'I thought he was going out with that Lara girl,' Sam said.

'Apparently not,' I said.

'So what's he really like?' said Charlotte.

He wasn't like you'd expect. He sometimes seemed quite

earnest and serious, but he was goofy and funny with me. He held my hand. He made lots of jokes. For our twenty-five-day anniversary, ('Silver Day', he called it), Wolfie took me to the seaside at Bridlington. It was overcast and grey, but that only seemed to make the town more romantic – there was none of the tackiness of the seaside when it's hot, no wet kids screaming and prodding you with gooey sticks of rock – just moody grey clouds and an amazing steely sea. We walked around the harbour – which smelled strongly of fish – and I leaned back on him and our gaze sailed over the waves out to the horizon. Wolfie had brought his camera, and he took some photographs.

'I love the sea,' I said. 'I wish I could always live somewhere close enough to walk to see it.'

'I love it too,' Wolfie said, squeezing my shoulder. 'It makes you think that no matter what we do to the earth, the earth still has the power to win.'

'Well, sort of,' I said. 'We're doing our best to poison the sea as well, pumping it full of chemicals.'

He kissed the top of my head. 'Just look at it, though. It's so *vast*. Can you believe that years before anyone had any idea what was out there, they set out in boats, sticking fast to one direction. They believed they'd find something and they were willing to die trying.'

'You'd have done that, I think,' I said, feeling slightly sad. I'd always been quite afraid of travel and leaving home, and I knew he wanted adventures. I hoped I'd be brave enough to go along with him.

'You love your family so much,' Wolfie said. 'It's very easy for you to want to stay close to them, because you know how much you'll miss them. I've always wanted to travel, because I've always been looking for something I haven't had. You're very lucky.'

Wolfie never really talked about his mum, and why she didn't live with them. I knew his parents were divorced, but I didn't know how often he saw her. Sometimes when he mentioned her it sounded as if he loved her very much, but other times it sounded as if he was very angry with her. On our Silver Day, I knew we knew each other well enough for him not to mind me asking.

'Where is she?' I said. 'Where does your mum live?'

'Scotland,' he said. 'Glasgow, actually.'

'How often do you see her?'

'About ten times as often as she wants to see me,' Wolfie said. 'I last saw her a couple of years ago, although we've spoken on the phone since then.'

'So . . . do you not get on?'

'I make my mum sad,' Wolfie said. 'She feels bad

about not being there when I was growing up and still not
. . . being there.'

'When did your parents divorce? Sorry, am I asking
too many questions?'

He kissed my head again. 'They were never married,'
he said. 'You remember you said you were expecting my
house to be really hippieish?'

'Yeah.'

'My mum was like a real flower child, except born
too late. She was a rich girl and she rebelled against her
posh school by getting pregnant at sixteen to a student,
and then leaving school to live with him. But when I was
born she couldn't hack it. You know, she was your age
and it was too much for her. She said she needed to feel
free again.'

'Maybe you get your sense of adventure from her,' I
said. 'What did she do?'

'She left me with my dad when I wasn't even a year
old. He had to drop out of college and get a job so he
could pay for babysitters.'

'I thought you said she was rich. Did she never send
you stuff?'

'Money on my birthday and at Christmas. You
know, quite a lot, although she didn't always remember,
because she was getting on with her own life.'

I hadn't turned around, because I didn't want to embarrass him by looking straight at him, but his voice had become lost and quiet, and I turned and met his eyes, which were shiny, and buried my face in his chest, hugging him.

'So why is she in Scotland?' I asked.

'She's got a new family, now, three kids, and I don't think she's interested in making me a part of it. Well, I know she's not. I mean, her new husband knows about me, I'm not some guilty secret, but I think I am a source of guilt for her. So she writes back if I write to her, and talks to me if I call her, but she doesn't ask me any questions, and she doesn't ask me to go and see her. So I don't write or call so much. Am I freaking you out, Tess? I don't think you bargained for the whole sob story.'

My eyes were full of tears, which I didn't let him see.

'Of course you're not freaking me out,' I said. 'I wish I could make you feel better, that's all.'

'Are you kidding?' Wolfie said. 'You make me feel amazing.'

'Oh, come on,' I said.

'Aren't you having fun?' he said. 'I mean, before I started depressing you we were . . .'

'I love it here,' I said. 'You're not depressing me. I'm really touched that you'd open up to me.'

'I love you,' Wolfie said. I didn't say anything, just looked at him and kept holding back my tears.

When it started to rain we went to the Sixties Coffee Bar for lunch. It was this half-cool, half-touristy retro café with pinball machines and old posters and displays. Wolfie had the veggie special, of course, the 'Hippie Feast'. I thought to myself how amazing he was, when his mum had hurt him so badly, to not reject her – he didn't try to suppress the aspects of his personality that were like hers. I was slightly self-conscious about eating meat in front of him, although he never said anything, or looked at me, or acted appalled, when I did. I didn't want to test him, but I wanted to know he'd still like me if I wasn't super-perfect, and that he'd still choose me if he knew the real me. I couldn't stop thinking about him saying he loved me, and me not saying anything back, even though I loved him too, and how weird that must have seemed to him and whether he regretted it, or meant it, and whether I should say something now. Anyway, I chose the 'Mod Revival', which was chicken and bacon and, when it came, it was just, you know, a sandwich. Sometimes I overthought things. The Coffee Bar played nothing but 1960s records, and we knew tons of them, and Wolfie sang along to a song called 'Concrete and Clay'.

He said it was one of his favourites.

After lunch, he took me to this mad place called the Beside the Seaside museum, where we got to sit in a Victorian train carriage, and then go into a 1950s boarding house. There were really freaky dummies all over the place which talked: some of them were funny and some of them scared the crap out of me. I liked Joe and Connie's Beach Bungalow, where the dummies were fat and frumpy and wore knotted hankies and funny swimming costumes and gossiped, but Grumpy Len in the boarding house was just plain creepy. Wolfie made me jump by seeming to wander away until I was spellbound by the dummies, and then suddenly coming up behind me, grabbing me and talking like Grumpy Len in my ear: I screamed. Some old ladies looked at us, a couple of them frowning, but one of them smiled. My favourite thing was the old slot machines, because there was a fortune-teller, which *also* scared me – why were old-fashioned seaside attractions so creepy? I mean, Punch and Judy? A squeaky little wife-beating puppet? So, anyway, I asked the fortune-teller machine what would happen with me and Wolfie, and I was genuinely freaked out while it buzzed and lit up and then it fed me a paper fortune that said, 'Your love will last'. This was especially weird because she was answering my actual question, and I could have asked anything.

Wolfie wasn't watching me, he'd taken out his camera again and was wandering around taking photographs of everything. I put the fortune in my purse.

We'd hoped the lengthy detour indoors would last as long as the rain, but, when we came outside again, it was really chucking it down. Neither of us had an umbrella, so we ran in the rain until we were soaking, looking for shelter. Then we just gave up and held each other around the waist as we walked and laughed hysterically at how wet we were. We walked along the sopping sandy beach, and Wolfie said it was much nicer in the rain, anyway, because the sand was firm and didn't get into your clothes. He was looking completely beautiful to me, his long hair clinging to his face in dark spikes, his wet T-shirt tight and shiny over his chest. We sat down on the cold, hard sand and looked out at the choppy waves as they swallowed up the rain, and Wolfie said, 'They keep poisoning the sea, but it keeps renewing itself.'

The rain lashed against my face and I screwed up my eyes. 'We might as well have gone swimming fully clothed,' I said.

'What are you talking about – this is just a light shower,' he said, and we started laughing again, and he lay back flat on the sand, and pulled me over on to him.

* * *

On the train on the way back, I was sleepy, and rested my head on Wolfie's shoulder while he read a newspaper. We were both still wet through and had to hold each other to keep warm.

'That thing you said earlier,' I whispered, lifting my head to look him in the eye.

'Oh, the I love you thing? You don't have to be afraid of that,' Wolfie said. 'I just do. No big deal.'

'Really, no big deal?' I said, teasing him. 'Well, it's no big deal that I love you too. It's, like, whatever, so what if I do love you, ho hum.'

'You don't have to say . . .'

'I love you,' I said again. I put my head back on his shoulder, and he held me more tightly, and picked up his wet newspaper again with his other hand, and I wished the train ride would last forever.

Chapter 10

♥

The DVD Matty and I had just watched was *The Breakfast Club*, an American high school movie made in the 1980s, having settled back into our Friday-night movie routine again over the last few weeks. We'd seen the film before – so many times, in fact, that we called it 'Brek' – but this time it seemed to mean more to me, because the main girl in it ended up going out with the long-haired school rebel, and it was the first time I'd seen it since I'd started going out with Wolfie. Matty was reading the pizza menu while I went through the DVD options – there weren't really any. All the best films had no extras; it was only the stupidest, geekiest films that came with tons and tons of deleted scenes and commentaries.

'How about the Meat Feast?' Matty said.

I just didn't feel like meat. I'd eaten at Wolfie's – or shared whatever he was eating when we were out – so many times and, while some of his creations were a bit *strange*, others were yum, and I'd started wondering how much I really needed or wanted to eat meat. Bacon excepted – there was really no substitute for a bacon sandwich, especially when you were feeling ill.

'How about that one?' I said, pointing at a spicy, green, peppery one.

'What, the Hot Green?'

'Yeah, what do you think?'

'Oh God, you haven't gone veggie as well!'

'Well, now and then, if I can. I mean, there's no point throwing meat on something just for the sake of it. And actually, you know, pizzas are absolutely the worst things to eat meat with, because the pizza places just store cooked meat all week in containers and then reheat it, and it can have all kinds of –'

'Tessa . . .'

I looked at Matty, because she sounded mad at me, and added quickly, 'Well, whichever one *you* want, then.'

She didn't say anything.

'What?' I asked.

'Does it occur to you that you're changing yourself too much, you know, for Wolfie?'

'I'm not doing it so he'll *like* me. I'm not doing it to keep him. *You* know that if you hang out with someone a lot you start picking up a couple of their habits. He's done the same with me. I've changed him too.'

'Really. How have you done that?' Matty asked; she still sounded sort of irritated.

'Is this a joke?' I said. 'OK, he agrees with me that some of his records, some of the hip hop, is quite sexist and he didn't use to worry about that as much.'

'But that's just being like *him*,' Matty said. 'You're just becoming extra right-on, more than you were before.'

'I was always like this, Matty,' I said. 'Has it occurred to you that I just didn't talk so much about it, because I wasn't as confident and everyone always told me it was lame?'

'Actually, no.'

'Well, has it occurred to you that you just didn't pay any attention to what I was talking about, because you always had your own stuff to talk about and it was always more important?'

I had gone *waaaay* too far.

Matty was silent for a bit longer.

'It's time I went home,' she said.

'I'm sorry, please don't,' I said. I bit my lip and we looked at each other. 'I didn't mean that at all. Really, I didn't. I just don't know why you're getting at me today.'

'I'm just worried about you,' Matty said.

'Oh my God, but why?'

'I just worry that he's changing you, and you're losing some of the person you used to be.'

'But Matt, I've never been happier, you know that? I'm in love and I have someone who understands me, and I know how to snog without practising on peaches . . .'

'Did you really *do* that?' Matty said.

'You told me it worked.'

Matty collapsed into giggles and, after a while, so did I. Soon, we were crying with laughter.

'And now?' she said. 'Do you still think it works?'

'Well, I . . .'

'If he's snogging you the same way a peach does,' Matty said, 'I think there might be something wrong.' We laughed harder, and Matty lay down on the carpet, and I thought the bad moment had passed. She stayed there for a while, quietly staring at the ceiling.

'It could be me,' she said. 'I could be worrying about myself and trying out my questions on you.'

'*You* haven't changed,' I said. 'You're still you and you're still my best friend and you always will be. Lee hasn't done anything to change you.'

'Maybe that's my problem,' Matty said. 'I look at you, and you've turned yourself into Wolfie's dream girl . . .'

'Really, I haven't,' I said. 'It's just that I seem to have more in common with him than I realised at first, and I love the way he makes me think about things. I like being good enough for him, because I respect him.'

'That's what I mean,' Matty said. 'I don't think I've tried hard enough with Lee, and I think he's got so many options, so many girls who'd do anything for him, that I . . .'

'He'd do anything for *you*,' I said. 'And he's lucky to get the chance to.'

'Please, Tessa,' Matty said weakly. 'I know Wolfie and you are really like *super cool*, but don't try and tell me that girls don't have to work a bit to keep boys, *especially* when you *so are*.'

Holy crap, Matty thought we were super cool? Wait a minute, Matty thought I was so *working* to keep Wolfie?

'It's really not like that,' I said. My head was spinning, trying to keep a hold of everything. I wanted to tell Matty she had the wrong idea about me and Wolfie, and the way we were together. I wanted to tell her she had the wrong idea about Lee, if she thought he could do better than her. At the same time, who was *I*, with my brand new first ever boyfriend, to tell *her* anything – she probably knew a lot more than me. Still, I just *knew* I was right about this, because there was no way Matty should have been with someone who made her feel insecure. And there was no way I'd feel the same way about Wolfie if he didn't seem to love and respect me the way he did.

We ended up compromising with a ham pizza and

watched a spoofy movie that neither of us found very funny.

'Do you think we should do something together?' I said.

'What are you talking about?' Matty said.

'You and me and Lee and Wolfie.'

Matty sighed. 'They're not really the same kind of guy,' Matty said.

'Yeah, I know,' I said.

'To be honest, I don't think they get on all that well,' Matty said. 'And they've known each other, or sort of known each other, for quite a while now.'

I wondered if Lee had said something nasty about Wolfie, because Matty seemed more certain that it would be a bad idea than me. I'd been around when Lee was making fun of him in the coffee shop, but maybe he hadn't stopped there.

'But if we were all together, you and me having a laugh, they might end up having a good time,' I said.

'Well . . .' Matty didn't sound convinced. 'Oh, you know what? Instead of making it some big deal, how about we all just hang out at Becca's party? Lee's coming, you're coming, so bring Wolfie.'

I thought this sounded like a brilliant idea. Matty and I really needed to feel closer again, and the thing, I thought, that might have been pushing us further apart was the fact that we were both spending more time with our boyfriends and less with each other. And there was no reason we couldn't combine the two things.

'Fantastic,' I said. 'It's going to be so cool.'

But I couldn't really interest Matty in making any all-new Lee-and-Wolfie plans. She said she and I would still have to go to the party together, because Becca's house was a car ride away, and Matty's parents were pretty strict about her going to parties: they thought they were drink and drug and sex and ritual sacrifice extravaganzas, and that they would lead to Matty being featured on *Crimewatch*. So it would probably be the tried and tested formula of her mum dropping us off and mine picking us up – the other way around, Matty's mum always came early and rang the doorbell, which Matty thought was social death – so we'd have to meet the boys there. Matty decided we'd have to get there first, too, because neither of the boys knew Becca all that well. I was much more excited than Matty: I could see a time in the near future where we got to hang out as two couples. I knew Wolfie wasn't that keen on Lee and, if I was being honest, I had a problem with him, too, but I trusted Matty, and Matty loved him.

'Listen, though,' Matty said, out of the blue, near the

end of the film, 'let's not make this a concrete plan. Lee's been a bit funny about stuff, recently. Just ask Wolfie if he'll come with you. Don't make it about the four of us.'

'Sure,' I said. 'Is everything OK, though?'

'Yeah-yeah, everything's fine,' Matty said.

I paused the DVD and went to get the ice cream. I knew there was probably something up, but, if Matty wasn't ready to talk about it, I knew from experience that I couldn't force her, and I didn't want to go back into our weird argument from earlier about whether I was changing too much to be like Wolfie. If I could influence the direction of the evening, my best bet was to make it all about ice cream.

It was Cookie Dough. It was good. The evening was saved.

Chapter 11

Then things got better. I was writing some course-work at home on the dining table straight after school. My mum wasn't home yet, my brother was on the other side of the room watching the telly, and my dad was tootling around in the kitchen making himself a sandwich before dinner. We heard a *commotion* outside the house, and my dad asked my brother to turn down the telly. Before he had, the doorbell rang and we could hear singing outside, and I realised it was Jane and Lara and Chunk and Wolfie. I ran to let them in.

'The Wood is safe!' Jane shouted.

They all started talking at once, and Wolfie came in first and grabbed me round the waist and picked me up.

'What?' I said. 'What's happened?'

'Come on, you,' Jane said. 'We're all going to run around in the Wood to celebrate.'

'The supermarket failed to get planning permission at the last meeting. All because of our brilliant . . .' Chunk said, until Lara interrupted him.

'Well, we don't *know* that it was our . . .'

'It can't have hurt,' Chunk said.

'Is it really true?' I said. 'Is it definitely safe?'

'Yes it's true!' Jane sang.

'OK, no time to waste,' Lara said. 'Come on, Tessa.'

'Can you come, Tess?' Wolfie whispered in my ear.

'Dad, is it OK? I'll be back for dinner,' I said.

'Sure,' my dad said, through a mouthful of cheese sandwich. 'Go on.'

We all tumbled out the door and ran to the woods. Wolfie and I walked a little behind the others. Once, Lara turned round to look at us, and she looked a little sad, and I felt bad, because it seemed so obvious that she had been wishing he'd ask her out, and instead he'd chosen me. I wanted Lara to like me. I was still very in awe of her, because she was so clever and talented and pretty.

'I can't believe it's really safe,' I said.

'It had to be your fabulous essay,' Wolfie said.

'Or your fabulous picture,' I said.

'Well, they chose the most boring one,' Wolfie said.

'They were all beautiful.'

'Well, the *most* beautiful one was . . .'

'Keep up, you two,' Chunk said, beckoning us on without turning round to look at us.

The woods were absolutely beautiful that evening because they were suddenly really ours; we'd saved them.

Well, us and all the older people who'd held the meeting and talked to councillors and mailed petitions and gone to the planning permission appeal. But we'd made a difference. There were lots of other people there, and everyone was saying hello to everyone else and asking if they'd heard, and nodding and saying that was why they were there. People had brought out their children and were walking with them through the trees, explaining that they'd been saved from bulldozers. Jane started talking to a little white-haired old man: she told him what we'd done and he'd seen our page in the local paper, and he said it was 'splendid, really splendid' and added, 'I know as an old git I'm duty bound to say that everything is changing too fast, but I've been walking by these trees my whole life, and it really didn't need to be swapped for another new place to buy one hundred different types of toilet roll.'

He shook hands with all of us before he left, and Jane gave him a little hug. I thought about how brilliant my new friends were, and then felt a little guilty that Matty wasn't sharing in this lovely moment when she was my best friend. I knew I'd have to tell her about it, and would probably downplay how exciting it was. I didn't want to gush, because it was the part of my life that most excluded her, and that made me feel bad.

* * *

When I got back, after a very quick snog with Wolfie in the garden, I went in to find my mum in a bad mood.

'Did you finish your work?' she asked me. She knew I hadn't.

'I'll do it now!' I said.

'Have you eaten?' Mum said.

I paused. I was starving. 'No,' I admitted.

'Your dinner's in the oven,' she said, 'although it's probably dried out now. It's nearly nine, you know? Eat first, and then see how much you can get done, but I *don't* want you going to bed late again tonight.'

'OK, I just have to . . .' I stopped.

'Just have to what?'

'I was just going to e-mail Matty to let her know the good news.'

'No,' Mum said. 'You'll start instant messaging each other, and you won't be done for another hour. I bet Matty has already done her coursework.' I shrugged. 'Tessa, I know it's the most amazing thing ever to happen ever . . .'

'But mum, I know you're not being serious, but it *is* seriously important and good and . . .'

'I know. But your GCSEs are really close, and every-thing you do now counts. Today is special, but in the near future, we're going to have to sit down and plan how many times a week you can see Wolfie, and how much time you can spend with Matty. You don't have that much spare time, you know?'

'Yes.'

'It's just a question of making a schedule and sticking to it, Tessa,' Mum said. By now she was being quite nice, although I didn't want to admit that her advice was sensible and everything she said was true.

The next day, as a *sort* of compromise, I asked if I could bring Wolfie home for dinner. Mum agreed, because she wanted to show that she wasn't being a monster and that she was willing to negotiate, as long as I had a sense of my obligations. Wolfie cooked, having the food ready just as Mum got back home. It was a really delicious olivey-potatoey-tomatoey stew, although Jack moaned that it needed bacon. My mum was totally charming and even a bit flirty with Wolfie, and she agreed to let him stick around to 'help' me with my homework for a couple of hours. The fact was, we had to be together that night, because it was our two-month anniversary.

'Sit down,' I told him in my bedroom. 'I made you something.'

He sat on my chair and I sat on his lap, and brought it from behind my back. While I was making such a big deal of it, I also worried for a moment that it might just be really lame. It was a mixed CD I'd burned for him, and all the songs were wolf-related. Well . . . some of them were pretty obscure, and some of them were a bit weird, because I'd sort of started to run out of wolves halfway through, so I just put on some of my favourite songs to fill it up. But before I had, there was 'Hungry Like the Wolf', 'Werewolves of London', 'A Wolf at the Door', 'A Man Ain't A-Nothing But a Wolf', 'Cry Wolf', and, um, 'After the Fox', which was this mad, funny movie sound-track song my dad always used to play.

Wolfie kissed me softly and sweetly.

'You're adorable,' he said. 'Stay right there.'

He pulled a little book out of his bag. I opened it up: it was made of thick card, lightly bound together and tied with a bow, and folded in baby-blue tissue paper. Wolfie had made a photo album of the pictures he took in Bridlington the day we went to the seaside. There was the Beside the Seaside museum with the creepy dummies, the Sixties Coffee Bar where we'd eaten, and loads of streaky-lens, moody, beautiful seascapes. But the pictures were so amazing, completely professional, black and white and really arty, with some soft-focus edging framing the details – an old lady laughing at a dummy that was virtu-ally identical to her, a tiny little girl hypnotised by the

Punch and Judy, and – oh dear – me with sopping wet hair laughing so hard you could almost hear me through the picture.

'They're like stills from a film of everything we did,' I said. 'They're incredible.'

'It was the day that was incredible,' Wolfie said. 'I just tried to take home as much of it as I could.'

'Thank you,' I said, looking into his gorgeous brown eyes. 'I wish I had a record exactly like this of every day I've spent with you.'

'Otherwise you'll forget?' he teased.

'Never,' I said. 'But I love this, and I love you. You're really *good* as well, you know?'

'You . . . well, it sounds cheesy, but you sort of inspire me,' Wolfie said. 'I didn't really know what I was doing until I met you. Do you really think they're not terrible?'

'Well, you might want to rethink the picture of the weird laughing girl . . .'

'You're beautiful,' Wolfie said, and when I put my hands in front of my face, because I knew it wasn't true, he gently moved them out of the way and kissed me. 'You're the most beautiful thing in the book.'

My mum knocked on the door to chuck him out at about

ten. She came in and sat with us for a bit and thanked him for cooking dinner and told him he could come and do it again any time.

'Men who cook,' she said to me when Wolfie had gone, 'are worth keeping around.'

'I'm glad you approve,' I said.

'He's nice to you,' Mum said. 'He appreciates you. That's really all that counts.'

I gave her a big hug.

Chapter 12

Not everything was working out so well.
Wolfie wouldn't go to Becca's party.

'Sorry, Tess,' he told me, over the phone.
'I'm watching the football with Chunk on Saturday.'

'*Football*?' I said. 'But that'll finish quite early, won't
it? And isn't it on every week?'

'It's the quarter-finals, so it's really important, and
I've got a pre-arranged thing with Chunk – we're going
to hang out afterwards,' Wolfie said. 'I'd love to go with
you, Tess, but you're going with Matty anyway, aren't
you?'

'Well, Matty and I thought we all might sort of hang
out as a couple of couples,' I said. 'Her and Lee and you
and me.'

'Me and Lee Kelly?' Wolfie said. 'Can you really see
that happening?'

'Can't you just . . .'

'He's a jerk, Tess,' Wolfie said. 'We both know it. I
like Matty, but life's too short to make small talk with her
jerk boyfriend. Look, you go, have a nice time with

Matty, answer the jerk back when he starts being a jerk and make me proud of you . . . then come back and tell me about it. We'll spend Sunday together, and you can celebrate with me – or console me – about the match.'

'I'm just worried that Matty and I are losing touch with each other, and I thought if we started . . .'

'Tess, Lee Kelly and I are not going to start liking each other just because we like you two girls. You'll have a good time without me.'

'But Matty'll be there with Lee and I'll be like a gooseberry again.'

'Then come and watch the football with me. You might end up liking it.'

'No. I've told Matty I'm going, so I'm going. Anyway, my mum's giving us a lift home – her parents won't take her both ways.'

'You'll have fun,' he said. I was sort of annoyed and didn't know whether I should come out and say it, as he obviously couldn't pick it up from my tone. I was also embarrassed about what I'd have to tell Matty. Her boyfriend would support her, mine was putting a football match ahead of a really important party. Maybe she was right – maybe I did do too much to please Wolfie.

'I'd have more fun with you there,' I said.

'Well, I'd have more fun with you if you change

your mind and come and watch the footie with us.'

'You know I won't,' I said, feeling tired. 'Are you . . .'
I trailed off.

'What?'

'Well, do you feel like we've been spending too much
time together?'

'*No,*' Wolfie said. 'I'm crazy about you, Tess.' He
said it quickly and quite quietly, so I worried it was just
something he felt he had to say, and I couldn't say anything back for a second. 'My dad's home,' he explained. 'I
don't think he's listening, but . . .'

'Why don't you get a mobile, then you can talk in
your room?' I said. 'They're this hot new invention,
maybe you've heard of them?'

'Yeah, I've heard of them,' he said, sounding more
amused, more like his usual self. 'You know I don't like
the idea of them, no one knows for sure what effect the
pylons are having on the environment.'

'Can't you use my pylon?' I suggested. 'I'm pretty
sure they won't put up a new one just for you.' Wolfie
laughed, but I was still frustrated and feeling a bit insecure.
I felt sure other girls' boyfriends were less hard work.

Matty didn't seem too bothered when I told her, although
I apologised again on the night of the party.

'Well actually, I don't know if Lee's coming now,' she whispered, as we got into her mum's car. She sat in the front and I was in the back, so I couldn't ask her any more about it until we were there, although I really wanted to know what was up. Her mum talked to me about GCSEs and said Matty wasn't doing enough work, and Matty sighed and looked out the window. She was wearing a high-necked shirt that I knew she'd be taking off as soon as she was out of the car. Matty often went out wearing two outfits.

'She spends too much time on the Internet,' Matty's mum said. 'I suppose she's in those chat rooms.'

'Mum! I'm right here!' Matty said. 'And no one goes in chat rooms. I talk to Tessa about work, and there are loads of specimen essays and things about the courses we're doing.'

'Is that true, Tessa?' Matty's mum asked me, shouting so I could hear her in the back, although I could hear her fine before.

'Yes!' I shouted back. Matty and I did sometimes pop into chat rooms, but we just did it to have a laugh, and to argue about silly things with people who had no idea who we were.

Becca let us in, looking pretty and a little bit tipsy, and I hoped Matty's mum couldn't tell from her car. She showed us to the big bowl of punch, and Matty, as I'd predicted, bundled her high-necked shirt with our bags, and reappeared wearing a beautiful green silk halter-neck that set off her shiny red bob amazingly. She was absolutely gorgeous. Wolfie made me feel pretty, in the way he looked at me, and by telling me I was, and just by being my boyfriend, and I had begun to feel more confident about everything since I'd known him, but when Matty was looking her best, I just had to stand back and admire her. It seemed wasted on Lee, who did show up, late, looking surly. He didn't compliment her; he just sat around, asking her to get him beer. My plan had been to look for the best in him tonight and tell Wolfie all about it when we met the next day, saying that *Matty's* boyfriend skipped the football to make her happy, and was really lovely to her. But the plan was going to have to change. Matty and Lee started bickering, without embarrassment, and without even seeming to care whether I was there, so I thought the best thing to do was to go and circulate.

Becca was singing karaoke by this time, which was really funny, and I started chatting to Jim Fisk, of tree-carving fame.

'She still arguing with him?' Jim asked me.

'Matty? Oh, did you see them?' I said. 'Yes, I don't know what it's about.'

'So how are you, these days?' Jim said. 'I haven't seen much of you since I moved. We take too many different classes, too. I hear you're a proper loved-up hippie now. I-love-nature, I-love-wolves . . .'

I laughed. 'I'm having a good time,' I said.

'I heard about you saving the Wood,' Jim said. 'I thought the thing you wrote for the paper was really good.'

'Thanks,' I told him. 'You're really sweet. Lots of people were sort of laughing at me, you know? I talked about fairies and stuff . . .'

'You could tell you meant it to be funny. And it was,' Jim said. I could see why I had once fancied Jim – he was lovely. But I'd moved on, and I didn't feel anything like that for him any more. I really was in love with Wolfie.

About an hour after he'd come, Lee went. He slammed the door, and Matty came in to find me.

'Shall we go?' she said. Her eyes looked strained and pink, and I could tell she was close to tears.

'Are you ready now?' I asked her. I wanted to give her a hug. But whenever anyone felt sorry for me it was guaranteed to make me cry and I didn't think Matty would want to cry in front of everyone, so I didn't ask her what had happened with Lee. I thought it would be better to wait till we were safely out of the party. 'I can call my mum.'

'Well . . . I'm just going to tidy myself up,' Matty said, and she headed for the stairs, where there'd been a small queue for the loo all night. I didn't know whether to follow her, thought about it for a bit, then told Jim I'd better see how she was. He nodded. I couldn't find her, and went back to the living room, where Becca was now doing a kind of dance routine to an old S Club number. I suddenly realised Matty had been taking ages and ages, and I knew I had to look for her again. Finally, I tracked her down in Becca's mum's bedroom, where she was sitting in the corner snogging a boy called Pete.

This was bad. This was really bad.

I got straight out and shut the door, because what else could I do? But my heart was thumping. For one thing, she was cheating on Lee, which was mega serious. For another, Pete, the boy she was snogging, was cheating on his girlfriend Kim, who wasn't there, but who was very scary indeed. If this got out, Matty would be in big trouble. I had to stop it before anyone else discovered them. I knocked on the door.

'Matty,' I said. 'I called my mum and she's on her way.' It wasn't true, but I could do it any time soon. There was silence from behind the door. I leaned against the wall and waited. Jim walked past and asked me if I was OK. I fudged things and said I was just waiting for Matty.

'She's in there?' he said. 'But didn't Lee go? Is he back?'

'Er . . . I don't know where she is,' I said. 'I'm just waiting here because it's nice and cool.'

'OK,' Jim said. He looked as if he didn't believe me, and he looked sad again. I thought he had been hoping her argument with Lee might give him the chance to comfort her.

Eventually Matty came out. She was drunk and smelled of smoke.

'Have you been *smoking*?' I said.

'Just one,' Matty said.

'But you hate fags. God, are you drunk?' I said. 'You look really drunk. You're pink and . . .'

'Hardly. Look, Tessa, are you my *mother*?'

'Matty, what the hell are you doing? Have you been in there with Pete? What about Lee? Where did he go?'

Matty started crying incredibly loudly and slumped down on the carpet.

'Matty, honey, what's happened?'

'He's dumped me. He said he'd met someone else and been out with her a few times, but he still loved me and he was trying to choose between us. I went mental and he said, "Thanks, you've made my mind up for me".'

'Oh my God! What an absolute *arse*!'

'Yes,' Matty said, and then cried a lot more. I stroked her hair. Pete came out, looking nervous, and then slipped off downstairs.

'Lee's a total idiot,' I said, pretending not to have noticed Pete. 'Look, my mum's not coming yet. Come and sit with me in the kitchen, and we'll make some coffee and you can . . .'

'Tessa, I'm so unhappy,' Matty sobbed. 'I love him so much.'

'Well, what were you doing snogging Pete?' I said.

'Did you see us?' Matty said. 'It's OK. He's not going out with Kim any more. He said they broke up. That's why she's not here.'

'Well, let's hope that's true,' I said. 'You don't fancy Pete, do you?'

'No, I want Lee back,' Matty answered, crying harder again. 'I just want to go back to where we were.'

I wanted them to go back to where they'd once been, too. When they first started seeing each other, Matty and Lee had seemed like the perfect couple to me, and to everyone else. He was so cool and good-looking; she was so pretty and brilliant; and, when he asked her out, we were both excited and happy. Matty had shown me some of his e-mails, and he said all the right things, and when they were out together, they really *fit*. He could be really charming and it was hard not to be swept away by his confidence. But recently, I'd been more worried about her – I think because I was less in awe of him now. I winced sometimes at some of the things he said, and the way she tried too hard to keep him happy. So I didn't want her to take him back, because it would never have been the same as the way they'd been at the start. Basically, he wasn't good enough for her. Matty, I think, was in too deep to see him for what he was. When you get your heart broken, you don't think straight – you just want to stop the hurt. Having everything go back to where it was seemed like the simplest way to do that. I sort of wanted to shake some sense into her, but I put my arm around her instead until she'd stopped crying, and then we fixed her face and called my mum. The party was still noisy with other people laughing and singing, but now it seemed like the most horrible place on earth.

Chapter 13

I woke up on Sunday morning to a bedroom splashed with sunlight, which seemed to dim as the grief of the previous night came back to me. Wolfie rang to make plans for the day, but I was still tired and emotional. Although I knew it was stupid, I was angry with him. I blamed him for not coming out, because when he was with me everything was safe and bad things didn't happen. And I was still feeling hurt about losing out to a football match. I wanted to see him and know we were fine, but a part of me was sulking and wanted to hurt him back, so I said I had to go round to Matty's to see how she was feeling. He heard the stiffness in my voice and asked if *I* was OK, and I said I was just worried about Matty and needed to spend some time with her. After I hung the phone up I felt silly and petulant and wrote him an e-mail full of kisses and expressed relief that he hadn't had to see his prejudices about Lee confirmed.

It turned out that Matty was going with her mum to see her granny in Liverpool. I checked the computer and Wolfie had already sent me a sweet, slightly anxious e-mail back, but I made my mind up not to call him even so. I just felt I needed a day off from normal life. Sometimes, even though you know someone will make you feel better, you just want to shrink away and hide and feel miserable and sorry for yourself in a completely self-absorbed way, a way you don't want other people to see. I spent the day at home, slobbing out, reading the papers and watching rubbish television, while all the time my mind wandered to the people I cared about.

If the party seemed like bad news, Monday at school was worse. During morning break, Matty and I were sitting near the school goat, talking about Lee. Matty had decided not to take him back, despite spending the rest of Saturday night crying and telling me how much she loved him. Since then, she'd become harder, but more fragile. She said she'd just been drunk and sentimental, and now she saw clearly what an idiot she'd been. I didn't agree, because I didn't think it was a good idea to dis your friends' boyfriends when they'd broken up. For one thing, there was always a chance they'd get back together – this had happened with Matty in the past – and for another thing, you never really knew what things were like between people, or why they were together, so there was nothing *you* could tell them that they didn't already know – better than you! – and I-told-you-so was no help to the person you'd told so, and any-way, how could you explain why you hadn't given them the advice at the time, if it was so important? So I watched the goat ambling around its little square and let Matty talk.

Then, Kim Brannigan, Pete's girlfriend, came round the corner with a couple of her girl friends, obviously looking for us. She was tall and square with dyed blond hair and was properly scary.

'Did you snog Pete on Saturday night? At that party?' she said.

Matty just looked at her, but I could tell she was afraid.

'Did you snog Pete?' Kim said. 'He says you did.'

'I . . . he said you'd broken up,' Matty said. She stood up to face Kim, and I stood up with her.

'We haven't broken up,' Kim said.

'I'm sorry,' Matty said. 'He said you had.'

I didn't say anything. I was hoping that now the mis-understanding had been cleared up, everyone would just get on with their lives. I knew there wasn't a cat in hell's chance that *would* happen.

'You're a slag,' Kim said. 'He said you just started kissing him after your boyfriend walked out. Like five minutes later.' She waited for Matty to say something, but Matty didn't. 'Quick turnaround. Who's next?'

Kim's friends didn't talk, either. They just glared at

Matty, and tutted, or snorted, when Kim spoke.

'I'm really sorry,' Matty said. 'I was drunk and I made a mistake. I thought . . .'

'Is that supposed to be an excuse?' Kim said. 'You're a drunk slag, so that's OK.'

'He told her he wasn't going out with you anymore,' I said. 'Do you think Matty forced herself on him?'

'If it's served up to him on a plate, he'll take it, won't he?' Kim said.

'Maybe you should be a bit more worried about him telling other people that he's single,' I said.

Matty looked at me, her eyes saying, 'Shhh'.

'This is *nothing* to do with you,' Kim snapped. I glared back at her, although I was terrified. I wanted my boyfriend. But this was my fight, my best friend, and I was staying right here. 'Lee Kelly's well shot of you, you slag,' she said to Matty. She seemed to be running out of ideas, and we had nothing else to say, so finally the three of them went away again, but I knew this wouldn't be the end of it.

As the week went on, I spent most of my time with Matty, not Wolfie, because she was so unhappy. Some girls had stopped talking to Matty, but everyone was talking *about* her. People whispered when she was answering questions in lessons; boys were making jokes about her. It was nasty. We got tired of the awkward silences when we went to join friends at lunch-time, so I took Matty to eat with Wolfie and his mates. Normally, he and I didn't have lunch together – he and his friends usually went out of school to his favourite veggie café, and I hung out with Matty and the girls, and Wolfie and I would occasionally spot each other and smile secretly, and maybe sneak in five minutes of snogging before classes started again. But today I thought Matty and I needed a break from everyone we knew.

I got it wrong. Wolfie's friends weren't very sympathetic, to say the least, and Chunk was even sort of making fun of Matty. When Jane said she was sorry to hear Matty had split up with her boyfriend, Chunk said, 'Which one was that? It's quite hard to keep up,' and there was silence, but Lara smirked a bit and Wolfie didn't say anything to defend Matty. I said we had to go, and Matty and I went back to sit with the goat.

'Everyone's being a jerk about this,' I said. 'So what if you snogged someone at a party? It's *his* fault. He told you he was single, and you were single, so what's the problem?

'God, it's a mess,' Matty said. 'I'm so screwed.'

'You're not,' I said. 'And I'm so angry!'

When I got home, I called Wolfie and asked him to explain himself.

'Explain what? What are you talking about?' he said.

'You and your stupid friends,' I said. 'Could they have been any less sensitive?'

'Well, in fairness to *us*,' Wolfie said, 'we don't actually care that much who your friend is snogging this week.'

'Matty has been going out with Lee for more than a year,' I shouted. 'Which is a lot longer than you and me. What's that supposed to mean: "*this* week"? Are you just saying the same things about her as everyone else?'

'Of course I'm not,' Wolfie said. 'Calm down, Tess. I'm just saying it's not very important.'

'It's important to Matty, and it's important to me,' I said. 'No one is talking to her, and she's incredibly upset. But as far as you're concerned it's nothing, because she's so *easy*, and you can't keep count of her one boyfriend in more than a year.' I was starting to shake with anger.

'You're really overreacting,' Wolfie said. 'I didn't say anything – it was Chunk.'

'Exactly: you didn't say anything!' I said.

'He was joking.'

'She's my best friend, and enough people are "joking" about her.'

'What do you want me to do about it now?' Wolfie said. I was silent. I couldn't think of anything to say. I just wanted him to make it all better, but I didn't know how, so I didn't say anything. 'Is it my fault she got pissed and made a fool of herself?'

'Is that really what you think?' I said.

'Well, I think she was making a fool of herself going out with that jerk Lee Kelly, but I think the fact she got over him *so quickly* was actually pretty cool,' Wolfie said, and I could hear him smiling at me, trying to make things better between us, but it was the wrong joke at the wrong time. We hadn't really sorted things out after we'd argued about him not coming to the party, and, with this happening so soon afterwards, I couldn't tell whether I was still hurt about that, and this argument was me still trying to work through it, or whether this was already another thing where we wouldn't meet each other halfway, and that it meant we had worse, more serious problems.

'I'm really mad with you,' I said. The thing was, even though I was upset and angry, I wanted to apologise at the same time for shouting at him, but I couldn't.

'Well, there's nothing I can do about that, is there?' Wolfie said. He and I held our phones in silence, until finally he said, 'Anything else?' and sounded annoyed, and I just stayed silent for ages and ages, and eventually he put the phone down. I hung up and burst into tears, somewhere between angry and hurt.

* * *

My dad and brother were out that night seeing a band play in Sheffield. I invited Matty round, and told Mum she was depressed, but I didn't go into things. Mum cooked us a really lovely risotto, and Matty ended up telling her about Lee and Pete and Kim. My mum told us about a boy she'd gone out with when she was our age. She hadn't slept with him, although he kept asking her to, and he told everyone she was a slag after she broke up with him.

'I hate that word,' Mum said. 'For a boy to use it, it's disgusting enough, but, for a girl to use it against another girl, it really makes me despair. And the only people who've behaved badly in all this are the boys.'

'Yeah, well, no one at school sees it like that, unfortunately,' Matty said.

'I don't want to sound as if I don't understand how serious this is,' my mum said, 'but I promise you it'll blow over as soon as it started, Matty.'

'I think she's right,' I said. I didn't tell either of them that it had led to my first serious fight with Wolfie. I still had to work out how I felt about it. He hadn't done anything *properly* bad, like Pete or Lee; he'd just stood around and done nothing while his friends had been mean to my friend. It *was* bad, sure, but did I really need to stop speaking to him over this? Was it unforgivable – a few careless moments? The trouble was, how did I go about getting back to where we'd been? How could we go from being so close and in love to suddenly not knowing what to say to each other or where to go next? I knew I wasn't angry any more. I just wanted him to have been sorrier and to have promised me nothing like that would happen again. I wanted him to promise over and over and hold me and reassure me until I didn't care any more. But at the time he'd just acted as if it wasn't important and tried to get past it. I wanted to be past it too! But with it all fixed, not swept under the carpet.

My mum, Matty and I carried on talking while we demolished a shop-bought chocolate cake, and I thought about how cool my mum was, and how lucky I was. Matty couldn't say anything like this to her mum, not just because she was her mum – *I* would never be able to talk to Matty's mum about anything except school work. But underneath the common-sense talk, right now, I was in a turmoil of my own. I didn't know what was going on. This was my first ever romantic fight. I had no idea what he was feeling and how it was going to turn out. And, although I was with people I loved and trusted, I just didn't want to talk to *anyone* about Wolfie yet. I kept quiet, because I didn't want to hear Matty or my mum tell me Wolfie was in the wrong. Or the exact opposite: I was afraid *I'd* messed up and didn't want anyone to confirm it.

Chapter 14

No Wolfie e-mails overnight, and none the next morning, Friday – although I wrote drafts of about a hundred and didn't send them. I made myself late with checking all the time for something from him, compulsively pressing 'get mail' 'get mail' 'get mail' when I was on the computer and jumping when the phone rang. I would have sent him a text: texts are good like that; because of the restricted space, you don't have to say anything, and you almost *can't* say anything. You're just sending them a sign that you *want* to talk, which makes it harder to mess up. But bloody Wolfie was living in the last century and refused to get a mobile. Anyway Matty's social catastrophe was still my offical first concern, and I found that being there for her made me feel better: it was good for me to remember I was not the only one with problems. I confessed to her that Wolfie and I had argued, although I didn't say it was because of the way his friends had talked to her. I just said it was over something stupid and Matty didn't ask any more. She just gloomily declared that all boys were a waste of time.

At lunch, Matty and I got chips and went to sit alone at the edge of the school field. The weather was starting to be reliably nice and there was hardly any breeze. We weren't social outcasts, or anything, but our friends spent a lot of time trying to ask us why Matty and Lee, the gorgeous couple, had broken up, and trying to get fresh juice. Matty was still hurting and didn't feel up to being everyone's daily entertainment. We thought it best that people knew as little as possible, so they'd have to find someone else to gossip about. Lee had told everyone about the other girl he was seeing, who went to a different school, and that was humiliating for Matty. But, with no chance of getting him back now, she decided to concentrate on work and take advantage of all the extra time she'd have not being with Lee. We lay back on the grass and looked at the clouds, and Matty said that, all things considered, it was an excellent time to break up. But I knew she was still hurting behind the bravado.

Matty and I went off in different directions when break was nearly over. She had to take back a library book and I wanted to check again for e-mail on one of the computers. When I saw Wolfie outside the science block, I panicked.

He didn't see me for a few seconds and when he did he froze. I wanted him to run up and hold me and tell me he was sorry, so that I could tell him it was me who'd overreacted, and that it was my fault we'd rowed, and he could say, no, no, until we met in the middle and everything was OK again. But, unless he made the first move, I was too afraid. If I ran up to him, he might reject me. Our last contact had been him hanging up on me when I stayed silent and nothing since then. He half-smiled and started to approach me. I couldn't work out his expression at all, and I was suddenly terrified that if I gave him the chance to come and talk, he'd tell me we were history. And I just wasn't ready to hear it. I turned around, even though I knew he'd seen me see him. I wanted him to come after me. I started to tremble with the anticipation of his touch – his hand on my side, pulling me back. But he didn't come. He didn't follow me.

By the evening, I started to believe we must be over. Wolfie still hadn't e-mailed or called me, so what else was I supposed to think? A simple phone call to him would have set my mind at rest, but it could also give me the very worst news of all, so I just put it off. I chickened out. I spent a quiet night in, *actually* studying and exchanging e-mails with Matty. Every time my e-mail bleeped to say there was a new message, my heart did somersaults. I could hardly tell Matty to stop e-mailing me, and I liked the breaks that reading her messages gave me. I hadn't told her that the situation with Wolfie had worsened, because she was upbeat and happier today, and it was great to see her starting to try to put Lee behind her. I didn't want to bring her down again, when even I didn't know where I stood. I still hoped there was another reason for him not being in touch. And the last time Matty had seen Wolfie had been *that* time, when his friends made fun of her, and she was in an 'all men are bad' state of mind, so she might not have given me the kind of advice I wanted.

On Wednesday morning, I'd just about given up. I didn't see him at all and he made no effort to come and find me. I felt everyone was looking at me – that they all knew what had happened, and they all thought I was a loser. I understood more deeply how Matty must have felt to have half the school talking about her and judging her, even though my situation was nothing like as bad as hers. Matty's private life had been everyone's business. In my case, the truth was that almost certainly no one knew anything about me or even knew I existed. I made a decision to keep it from Matty for another day, and to e-mail Wolfie when I got home. If he thought we should break up, Matty and I could be heartbroken together. But Matty was defiantly upbeat and had been flirting with Jim Fisk all lunch-break. Lee came round the corner when

Jim and Matty were laughing, opened his mouth to say something and then skulked off. Ha! I thought. You can see what you've lost, and you're sorry, and there's nothing you can do about it. Then I thought about how I could say the same thing to myself, and felt depressed.

When we were queuing for the bus home, I got a text from an unknown number.

COME TO CADEBY WOOD TONIGHT AT 7. PLEASE. W

But it couldn't be from Wolfie. He didn't have a mobile. He hated mobiles. Was someone setting me up for some horrible joke? I texted back:

IS IT YOU?

The reply came ten minutes later, when I was actually on the bus.

YES. PLEASE COME.

Well, there was proof. Good thinking, Tess – 'Is it you?' – because if someone was playing a trick on me they wouldn't dare *lie*, would they? Duh. Sometimes I amazed myself with my own stupidity.

But who would play a trick? And there was something about the plainness of his texts, the non-text-speak, that I trusted. He e-mailed like that too, without using abbreviations and numbers – it was one of the things I liked about him. At quarter to seven I told my mum I was going to meet Wolfie. I'd told her a little about our argument and she'd reassured me, telling me that I'd been right to challenge him.

'The fact that you have principles is probably one of the things he loves about you,' she'd said. 'If he's got anything about him, and I think he has, he'll be grateful that you stand up to him.'

'Grateful?' I said. 'And I'm not sure I stood up to him. I think I went crazy on him.'

'Matty's your best friend,' Mum said, 'and she came first.'

This had made me feel better: stronger. I might have been overreacting, but I was doing it for the right reasons.

'Why isn't he coming here to pick you up?' she said, when I was putting my jacket on.

'Oh, I . . . it's still light, Mum.'

'It doesn't matter if it's light,' Mum said. 'Be careful. Have you got your phone?'

Of *course* I had my phone. The mysterious texter could text back any minute. But I *knew* it was him – I just knew. When I got to the edge of the wood, I sent another message.

WHERE AM I SUPPOSED TO GO, ANYWAY?

The reply came faster this time.

YOU'LL SEE ME. HAVE A LITTLE FAITH.

I started writing another message.

SINCE WHEN HAVE YOU HAD A PHONE? WHOSE PHONE IS THIS?

But before I could press send, I saw lights twinkling through the trees, and then a little tent surrounded by a circle of tiny tea-light candles in little terracotta holders, set in a clearing. I held my breath: I was afraid to approach. I didn't know whose tent it was. Then I heard music, my wolf songs compilation, and I walked with confidence and love and my heart beating so fast I thought I might faint.

'Since when have you had a phone?' I said.

Wolfie stuck his head out of the tent.

'Trust you to spoil the mood,' he said. 'Come in.'

I stayed still where I was.

'Please?' he said. 'I know I've blown it with you, but come and sit down and tell me. Face to face. Let me have a chance to look at you one more time while you tell me what a jerk I am. We've been through too much for you to just break up with me by running away.'

I didn't move.

'I haven't broken up with you,' I said.

Wolfie came out of the tent and walked closer.

'You turned your back on me,' he said.

'I didn't know whether you'd want to talk to me.'

'I always want to talk to you.'

'I didn't know what you wanted.'

'I was an idiot,' he said. 'I let my friends let your friend feel bad. Why wouldn't you turn your back on me? For all I know you hate me. Do you?'

'You're not angry with me?'

'Are you kidding? *Me?* King of the Jerks?'

'Well, I was mad with you, yes . . .' I said.

'Of course you were,' Wolfie said. 'And? Go on? Let me have it. I deserve it. But first, wait . . . I bought you dinner . . .'

He reached back into his tent and presented me with a little foil-wrapped parcel.

'Dinner?' I said. I opened the parcel and it was a

lukewarm bacon sandwich, the bread soaked through with grease. It looked kind of delicious.

'I'll do whatever you want if you forgive me, Tess,' Wolfie said. 'Look at me: I'm wired up to a mobile phone network – Pay as You Go. Lara explained it to me – Lara feels quite bad, by the way – and I want you to eat meat. I don't want you to change anything about yourself, and I want you to know I'm willing to change everything to get you back. I'm all new now. I'm modern!'

I poked the sandwich.

'Where did you get this?'

'My dad made it.'

'Your dad's a good man. How *is* your dad?'

'He's very well, thank you. How's the sandwich?'

I took a bite.

'Oh my God, you're not really going to *eat* it?' he said, pretending to be horrified.

I mock-glared at him. 'You brought it for me!'

'Just kidding.'

'It's good.'

'I'm glad. Pig-eater.'

'Yeah. It's good pig,' I said.

'Well, if you can put that pig in your mouth, I'm hoping you might consider kissing this one,' Wolfie said.

'You're not a pig,' I said. 'You're a wolf.' He pulled

me close to him, and I felt my knees start to tremble and my head kind of cave in on itself, and suddenly he was kissing me, and I was holding him tighter, and he was stroking my hair and whispering that he loved me in the curve of my neck, and I was so happy I wanted to cry. A love song swelled in the background, and we danced slowly and kissed in the candlelit woods.

'I thought I'd lost you,' Wolfie said.

'I thought you never wanted to see me again,' I said.

'I always want to see you,' he said. 'I want to see you always. Please, Tess, let me make it up to you.'

'But I was never . . .' I paused. 'And I don't want you wired up and pig-eating . . .'

'Aiding and abetting pig-eating. *I'm* not eating it.'

'. . . I just want *you*. So . . . why don't you show me around your tent?'

Chapter 15

I f I could choose one month of my life and live in it forever, it would be that month, from that moment in the woods. As summer drew nearer, the revision schedule brought us close to cracking. I was studying for GCSEs and Wolfie for his A-levels. The overworking made us tired and stupid and giggly, but we were so close – not just me and Wolfie but everyone. Chunk, Jane, Lara and Wolfie were writing long A-level course pieces and panicking about getting their grades for university. Their work was hard because it really *really* counted. Ours was hard because, apart from its importance, there was such a gigantic spread of subjects to revise. At the weekends, or in the early evenings, Matty and I had started working at my kitchen table with a large jug of freshly squeezed lemonade, if we were feeling sunny and swish, or a six-pack of Diet Cokes, if we were feeling tired and lazy. Other days I'd work in the Wood, where I read propped up on my elbows on a rug, wearing a jumper because it wasn't *that* warm yet. Wolfie would lie on his side next to me, occasionally interrupting my concentration to talk about something in his book that bugged him or made him laugh, or lazily tugging at my hair when he wanted to be kissed. I started to love the routine as much as I hated the work. I liked being so focused and having someone there to support me. Sometimes we barely said a word all day, but it was always easy, and tender, and perfect.

It was a real relationship. I'd somehow managed to fall into this on my first time out. There was so much ahead and so much to look forward to. I used to wake up in the morning, my head hurting from the coffee and the concentration, and I'd remember everything that was good about my life and a lovely warm feeling would spread over me.

But there were things we didn't like to talk about. Wolfie was close to finishing school. His friends would be going to uni. He would be going to uni. He'd applied to do a degree in politics, but he'd started to doubt whether it was what he really wanted to do, and we both worried about what it would mean for us. Depending on where he got into, could I apply to the same place, and would I do that, when he'd already have been there for two years? Would my mum ever let me make such an important decision on the basis of a romance, no matter how much she understood that I cared about Wolfie? I didn't dare risk asking her yet: I just said Wolfie and I were working things out and wanted to do everything we could to stay together. And Wolfie and I didn't discuss it much: I held back, because I didn't want him to think of me as hard work, and I was scared that just *maybe* I was the one who thought it would be for ever, and he was more practical and see-what-happens about us. It was impossible to be totally rational, though. These choices would really change our lives, and it was the worst, most horrible luck that we had to make them now, when we were brand new and all we wanted was to be together.

But when Wolfie talked about us, the things he said gave me hope. He talked about random events in the future – like holidays we'd take together. Once we were on a bus, and he whispered, 'Look at that kid!'

I looked. A ten-year-old boy with chin-length hair and tatty jeans had sat down with a bigger kid on the seats opposite us.

'He's our son,' Wolfie said.

'What?'

'If we had a kid, that's how he'd turn out.'

I looked again. I saw what he meant. He had Wolfie's soft, full lips, and my flat, silky hair. My round face and Wolfie's scruffy dress sense. And just a look about him that made the idea funny and true. I elbowed Wolfie, who was shaking with laughter.

'Not yet, thank you,' I said.

Is it possible to meet the love of your life at sixteen? On your very first go? Some girls at school were engaged, or had made plans with their boyfriends to get engaged on their eighteenth birthdays. *They* believed it would work. People of my parents' generation got married early and sometimes stayed together. True, most people I knew expected to have lots of boyfriends before they settled down, and I had always thought the same way. If there was such a thing as true love and one special person, though, why shouldn't he be as likely to come walking into my life this year?

And what if he walked straight out again?

The first I heard about Peru was from Chunk, who was joke-flirting with Jane and asking if she'd wait for him. She played along, but I thought maybe, underneath it all, he wished she wasn't joking.

I said, 'What's this about?' and, when he told me, it became obvious that he'd talked about it to Wolfie before then. This was the plan: Chunk and Wolfie had kept in touch with someone called Adam, who used to work at Chunk's dad's paper. Adam had left the paper, gone to work down south and was now a freelance foreign correspondent for national newspapers. He wasn't much older than Chunk and Wolfie; he'd left school at sixteen and hadn't gone to university. He was involved with a bunch of independent charity workers who had been working in South America. He was so *good*, but as far as I was concerned he was a bad influence. Chunk and Wolfie loved him – they thought he was the coolest. I met him a few times: he was quite sophisticated and dry and patronising, and he'd lost his northern accent. He was going to leave for Peru in the summer and stay a few months there, writing about and working with people in an area that had been hit by natural disasters – there had been flooding and mudslides that had devastated communities. He suggested to Chunk and Wolfie that they could go with him. They'd be spending time helping people who were trying to rebuild their destroyed villages with actual physical labour, and at the same time he'd said Wolfie would be able to get invaluable photojournalism experience, if he was really interested in doing something like that. And of course Adam had the contacts.

'The whole summer?' I asked Wolfie later, hoping it would just be a couple of weeks. My heart sank: this summer might be all I had left with him. If he went to uni at the end of September, I'd barely spend any time with him from now until Christmas, and by then everything could be different.

'I need to find out more about it,' Wolfie said. 'But I was thinking, maybe it might turn out to be a good thing for you and me if I did go.'

'What do you mean?'

'Chunk's been thinking of deferring going to uni and I think I should do the same. It might be possible for us to stay on longer with Adam, which would make it a real reason to take time out before university. I could make it a proper gap and take the whole year out – stay in town, get a job, and hang around annoying you all year.'

'But I'll lose you now!'

'Yeah. That's the thing,' Wolfie said, and rested his head on my shoulder. I started to cry and hoped he couldn't tell. It wasn't just the thought of the immediate future; it was about everything that made me worry so much, about us changing. With the pressure of the exams higher than it had ever been, this was all too much for me. I stayed silent, because I didn't want my voice to crack.

'How are you feeling?' Wolfie said. 'Talk to me.'

'I don't like not knowing what's going to happen. I wish we could just go on the way we are now.'

'Me too,' Wolfie said. 'If I could take a year off just to follow you around, I'd have the time of my life.' He scraped his hand back from his forehead, flattening his hair. 'But I have to think about what I'm going to do for the rest of my life.'

'What *are* you going to do?'

'I don't *know*. I've always wanted to be a photo-journalist, but I didn't think people like me got to do stuff like that. But if I had A-levels already and a . . . like a portfolio, and I turned out to be any good at it, maybe I could apply next year for something like that. I never had any idea what I'd do with a politics degree.'

'Your dad's never going to let you go, though, is he?' I said, hoping this might be the barrier I secretly wanted.

'Maybe,' Wolfie said. 'Probably. You know my family – they're a lot more hands-off than yours.'

The idea was there and it was all I could think about, although Wolfie had told me to try to get back into revision, and not worry too much. He forced me to work an extra hour every time I was ready to give in and snog him and he was really sweet to Matty, taking time to get to know her, and apologising to me for having underestimated her.

'She's fantastic,' he said. 'Like you. She knows every-thing about music and films – I feel quite stupid when I talk to her. She has, in fact, taught me that people from that, you know, "super-cool" crowd can be actually cool.'

'Well, she's in my crowd. Did you used to think she was shallow or something?' I said, narrowing my eyes, but inside I was smiling all over. They were the two most important people in my life, and I'd always wanted them to really get each other, and had always worried that they wouldn't.

'Oh, she's incredibly *shallow*,' he joked, 'but she's a good egg. She'd cancel a hair appointment if you needed her. She'd give you her last Prada lip balm.'

I hit him playfully. 'But she would!'

'I know,' Wolfie said. 'I mean it. And I don't really think she's shallow – I think she's really funny. Intentionally and unintentionally funny. You and she are going to have a fantastic summer.'

I knew he hadn't meant to say it, but I knew that it meant he'd decided. He saw my face and understood.

'It'll go like that,' Wolfie said desperately, snapping his fingers. 'We'll be in touch the whole time. But I'll miss you like I'd miss breathing.'

I looked deep into his brown eyes, and he frowned and smiled at the same time. And I suddenly got it: I knew why he wanted to go, and I knew how proud I'd be when he came back.

'I know,' I said. 'I'm glad you have this chance and I want you to take it.'

'I love you,' Wolfie said. 'Love like this lasts.'

Chapter 16

We had two mid-week days off together halfway through our exams and Wolfie said we needed to take a full day's break to clear our heads. I thought my mum would just say no, but to my amazement she agreed.

'You've been doing the work,' she said. 'A day off may help it to settle in your head. And you can revise tomorrow. But by now you need to take it a little easier, he's right. You want to be making sure you're healthy, mentally healthy, not cramming more in.'

So books were banned, as was listing history dates and physics formulas. It was hard to get my head to stop at that point. I was dreaming English quotations. Equations rolled in front of my eyes as I was falling asleep. Wolfie turned up at nine a.m. and chatted to my brother while I got my things together. He'd been trying to get Jack into one of the bands he liked, and Jack was asking him about their latest album.

'Where are we going?' I shouted, wondering whether I should wear sandals or trainers.

I heard them laughing at me.

'Hurry up!' Wolfie shouted.

'Well, will there be walking involved?'

'No, I planned to pull you everywhere on a skateboard,' Wolfie shouted again. 'What do you think?'

'But what *sort* of walking?' I called again.

Wolfie came upstairs, and shut my bedroom door behind him. He folded his arms and stared hard at me.

'You don't understand,' I said, turning back to my wardrobe. 'Girls don't just have one pair of shoes. We have shoes that look good but hurt. We have shoes that don't hurt but don't look good . . .' He didn't say anything, and I looked at him again. 'What?'

He lowered his chin and looked up at me. 'Hi, you,' he said.

I smiled. 'What?'

He took a step towards me.

'Yes?' I said, mock-innocent. 'What do you want?'

He slid his hand around the small of my back. We kissed. We kissed a lot.

As we walked together towards the bus stop, I asked Wolfie what he wanted to do today.

'Well, you've got a few choices,' he said. 'We could get a train to York, and go wandering around the little streets there – the Shambles. It's very cute and olde worlde. Nice tea shops. We could see a film. There's a photography exhibition in . . .'

'You know what?' I said, looking up at him. 'Can we do nothing? We're both studied stupid. How about we just walk and talk rubbish and hold on to each other? I don't have you here for very much longer.'

'Good plan,' he said.

And we *really* talked. We'd both been under so much pressure that we hadn't just let ourselves go for such a long time – both of us had been too worried about upsetting the other or making things hard. Even more, we were both worried about making our last weeks together sad. Neither of us wanted that – we were both desperately trying to make sure we had a good time during every minute. But, in trying so hard, we'd started to kind of lose sight of enjoying ourselves. Wolfie and Chunk had been trying to organise their time around revision, research, contacting universities to ask about deferral, and talking to Adam about how they'd get to Peru and where they'd stay. Wolfie's mum had agreed to pay Wolfie's air fare.

'How did that go?' I asked him. He smiled a bit too bravely.

'Really good,' he said, nodding. Then he sighed. 'Ah, you know, me and my mum, we never quite match up. I don't think she really thinks of me as hers. And I sort of worry that every time we let a year go by without seeing each other, like we just have, that it makes it easier for her to let go. One day I'm going to be thirty and she's going to have missed, you know, my whole life. And it's not a bad life. There are some bits of it I'm sort of proud of. Everything that's happened this year . . .'

'If she didn't care, she wouldn't be helping you,' I said. 'She doesn't have to, you know.'

'Yeah . . .' Wolfie said thoughtfully. 'I want you to meet her, sometime.' He squeezed my sides. 'Not to . . . I mean, just so you know where I'm from. The thing is, I think you would like her.'

'When you get back, maybe,' I said.

'Do you know how much I'm going to miss you?' Wolfie said. 'I'm going to stay up late every night talking to Chunk about you, and wish he was you.'

'Yeah, I know,' I said, forcing my mouth into a smile. I didn't want him to see me upset about this today.

We bought lollies from an ice cream van, that turned our tongues bright pink. We read the jokes on the sticks to each other. We made up stories about people who walked past. We played guessing games with film and music clues. We found a little bench in the garden of a church-yard, and I rested my head on his shoulder, and we sat quietly for ages until the sky started to turn pink. And, on this day of doing nothing, I thought I'd never felt so old and so young before. In some ways, I didn't feel ready for everything that was happening around me, but at the same time I wanted desperately to move on to the next level, where – it seemed to me – I'd have some space to relax. What I mean by this is, where I was now it felt like everyone else was making all my decisions for me, and for the first time in my life I felt ready to make those choices myself.

As he walked me back home, we went down a street I never usually walked down, and I told him a story about when I was really little and I followed a marching band or street procession or something, I didn't really remember who they were, only that they were going past my house, and I got lost and knocked on someone's door to ask them if I could call my mum, and a horrible old man answered, and just stared at me for a minute and then shouted, 'BOO!' and I ran all the way home in tears, somehow finding the right way back. But, ever since then, I'd been scared of that door, although I was only half sure it was the same one.

'This door? Do you want me to tell the old man off for you?' Wolfie said.

'No! You can't go bullying old men!' I said.

'Yeah, sure . . .' he teased. 'He made you cry. I'll sort him out.' He mimed going to knock on the door, and I pulled him back by the arm, balancing on my heels and giggling hysterically. At last he stopped, and we carried on going home, leaning on each other.

'I suppose he might be dead by now,' I said, feeling sad – sometimes when I felt most happy I felt sad at the same time. 'I never told my mum, because I knew she'd go mad if she found out I'd knocked on a stranger's door. But I used to pull her away when she tried to take me down here.'

'I love it when you tell me things you haven't told anyone else,' Wolfie said.

'Really?' I said.

'Yeah. It's like you've let me know the real you,' Wolfie said. 'You know, it's kind of really special . . . that you trust me, that you feel you can tell me anything or talk about anything – you're not holding part of yourself back.'

'Tell me something you've never told anyone else.'

'I love you.'

Chapter 17

The end of exams brought a lot of parties and I went to all the official ones with my year. I stayed up through all the late nights and celebration, although I was used to being quiet and coupley now, and a lot of the time I just wanted to be home alone with Wolfie. But not everyone in my year would be staying on for A-levels, and this was precious time for us. The fact that we would be going in different directions made all my friendships feel suddenly closer. In the future, the truth was, we'd have to make an effort to stay in touch, which was something we'd never had to do before. There was a lot of crying and hugging and promising to be friends for ever, and I thought that, as painful as *this* was, it was nothing compared to what would be happening in a week between me and Wolfie. One important difference would soften the blow: we knew we'd be together again before the year was over – he would be back in the autumn. But I found the thought of separating from my new friends, Lara and Jane, very painful too. When I was growing up, I often sort of felt I was in the wrong crowd.

I had some good friends, but I never felt right at the centre of the gang; I wasn't quite, you know, *settled* with them. I sometimes felt myself pretending to laugh at things I didn't find funny, or making out I liked bands or TV programmes more than I really did. But, with Lara and Jane, although I'd been intimidated by them to begin with, I felt they were much more on my wavelength; we had more interests in common and seemed to think the same things mattered. I knew we'd stay in touch because of Wolfie, but, in a way, I hoped they thought of themselves as my friends – because of who I was, not because I was their friend's girlfriend. As they were going straight to university, not taking a year off like Chunk and Wolfie, they wanted to spend as much time with the boys as they could and, although Wolfie and I wanted to spend time on our own, we wanted to see them too. That was how we ended up spending our last night together with everyone.

It was Jane's idea to go camping. It would just be the five of us – Matty didn't want to go. In the after-exam parties, Matty and Jim Fisk had started to become a sort of item – perhaps it was more like friendship to begin with, when Matty was still getting over Lee, but lately it hadn't been looking all that platonic. I hadn't seen this coming and I was really pleased for both of them. Jim seemed to be happier about it than anyone I'd ever seen. When they were out together, he couldn't stop looking at her – he was absolutely devoted. Matty, who'd been going out with Lee for too long, and had got used to him comparing her to other girls, was swept off her feet by Jim's sweetness. I didn't have much hope of attracting a girl like Matty to a night of lying in a rock hard field being eaten by flies, and Matty's mum was dead against it anyway. Really, I just wanted to make sure she didn't feel left out, because a few months before, when Wolfie and I were just starting out and she was coming to the end of her relationship with Lee, we'd sometimes found it hard to understand each other. It had shaken us both up. Now, we were beginning to get back on track – but more than that, we'd really started getting each other more and growing closer. Because I'd never had a boyfriend before, we'd always had the kind of friendship where Matty seemed to do all the living, and I advised her and loved hearing her stories, but didn't really take part in the same way. These days we learned from each other and supported each other, and our friendship was once again one of the best and the most important things in my life.

'You and I have all summer,' Matty said. 'You'll be sick of me soon enough. Make sure you and Wolfie get away from the others, though. He's *your* boyfriend, and you need some time. And give him my love.'

Chunk was allowed to borrow his dad's car to take us to the field we were camping in, which was in the Peak District. My mum knew everyone, but she wasn't mad about us being driven by someone so young and inexperienced, and demanded to have a word with him before we went – this involved her practically testing him on the entire Highway Code. I was incredibly embarrassed – Wolfie and the girls were making fun of him behind her back, as he stuttered his way through stopping distances. She also gave us a big stack of tupperware boxes of food, told me about thirty times to phone if we had any problems, and kissed me a lot. On the surface, she was so much cooler than Matty's mum, but when it came down to it, mums were mums. Eventually, I just resigned myself to it, and let her go ahead, realising there was no point shrugging off her affection just to try to look cool.

'My mum used to be the same,' Lara whispered, when the car doors were shut.

The boys put up the tents. They wanted to. Lara, who'd been a Girl Guide and who, she revealed wickedly, had put up Wolfie's tent for him the night he and I got back together, laughed quietly at them for doing it wrong and predicted the point when they'd admit they needed our help. The three of us girls were giggly and close, lying on our backs and watching the sun turning gold as it started to set, and I didn't feel nervous at all with them, or young, the way I once had.

'Thanks for letting us share him tonight, Tessa,' Jane said. 'You could have dragged him off for a private romantic evening. We're going to miss him too. Both of them.'

'No, we've really been looking forward to tonight,' I said. 'And how lucky are we with the weather? It's the most beautiful night of the year. It's perfect.'

'You'll still hang out with us this summer, without Wolfie, though?' Lara said.

I paused before answering.

'I know I've sometimes been a bit frosty with you,' Lara went on, 'but I was just annoyed with you for really pathetic reasons. I . . . Jane?'

'Well . . . we've got a bit of a confession. And it's definitely not true any more, so don't worry. Lara was *sort of* annoyed at you for stealing Wolfie from me for a *tiny* bit,' Jane said. 'But he and I were never going to make a go of it.'

'Before we *knew* you, though!' Lara said quickly.

'*You* fancied Wolfie?' I asked Jane. I was feeling sort

of sick and scared, because everything I'd believed about Lara had been true – she really hadn't liked me much for a while, though I'd thought it was because *she'd* liked Wolfie, not *Jane*. I sort of wanted to curl up and die, all my early fears of annoying them flooding back. More importantly, if Wolfie had known how Jane felt, would he have fancied her? Might we never have gone out? But I knew he loved me and these were crazy insecure things to think.

'Well, for a bit,' Jane said. 'But you know, in a really stupid way. I didn't do anything about it, and he always thought of me as a sister, and I feel the same about him now. He's like my brother, I mean. And I've fancied other people since him and I . . . but you know, Lara just thought you came out of nowhere, and she . . .'

Lara took over. 'I just thought you were a bit of a twinkie, you know? Sort of an airhead.' I didn't feel insulted, because she was grinning, her voice ready to crack up, and Jane was starting to giggle. 'Because you're so pretty and trendy, and I always thought Wolfie and Jane would end up together. I was totally wrong – you're fab. And Wolfie's so into you. God, I was stupid.'

Because she was making fun of me, I felt better. Do you know what I mean? She was relaxed enough to not come over all sugary and apologetic. I did like Lara's bluntness. When people are straightforward, it's easier to tell when they really mean something. She propped herself up, raising her eyebrows as she looked at me, careful to make sure I knew she wasn't being hurtful. She was smiling and laughing, and soon, so was I.

'Pretty and trendy, me? Are you crazy?' I said. 'Have you *seen* Jane?'

'Yes, Jane's beautiful, but I always knew how deep Jane was ... you, I thought ...' Lara laughed. 'I'm actually insulting you again. Look, I get it now. I was an idiot.'

'Hey, even *I* thought I was an airhead,' I said, laughing. 'God knows what Wolfie saw in me.'

'We all know what Wolfie saw in you,' Lara said. 'You're great.'

'Yep,' Jane said, nodding. 'I always liked you anyway,' she joked, looking pointedly at Lara.

'Well, you're both great too,' I said. 'And if Wolfie really thought of *you* like a *sister*, he's stupider than even Lara thinks.'

Right on cue, one of their tents collapsed, and we all looked up and saw the two boys hidden in its folds, and laughed again.

'No, but he and I have always just been friends,' Jane said, taking my hand and squeezing it. 'I swear.'

'Thank you,' I told her.

* * *

The guys joined us for the sunset, which was spectacular. We lay side by side watching it deepen and soften, then the stars began to show, then the sliver of a new moon. Chunk talked about how he was terrified of flying, and Wolfie talked about how much he'd miss all of us. He kind of choked up when he mentioned me, and stopped talking and rubbed my neck. Chunk and Jane and Lara kept on talking, and Wolfie and I looked at each other, and right at that moment I believed we knew exactly what the other was thinking. My eyes filled with tears. I suddenly had this horrible feeling of falling. I felt lost and sad and afraid of losing him forever, and I could see the same thing in his eyes. It was just incredibly intense: we wanted to hold each other really tightly, but we were still with everyone else, and we couldn't. I thought about the way we'd spent that day together doing nothing and still not wanting it to end, and how for months and months to come, I'd be doing nothing *without* him.

'I'm not worried about us,' I said to him later, when we slipped off for a walk over the hillside on our own. 'Remember Silver Day? I didn't mention this at the time, but actually I consulted a fortune-teller, and . . .'

'When? Oh, not that creepy machine in the penny arcade?'

'Yes.'

'I saw you looking at that. I thought you were afraid of it.'

'I was. That's why what she said must be real,' I said. 'She was too scary to be just a machine.'

'So what did she tell you?'

'I'll show you,' I said, smiling up at him. I looked for the crumpled little slip in my purse, but it wasn't there. I'd lost it sometime without realising it.

'Oh my God, it's gone!' I said. 'It said our love would last. Honestly it did. Oh no, do you think that's a bad omen?'

'Well,' Wolfie said, putting his palms out, pretending to weigh up the possibilities in his hands. 'On the one hand, you had that very important piece of documentation saying our love would last . . . but you've lost it. That *is* pretty serious. On the other hand . . . I'm completely *nuts* about you, you superstitious looney!' He put his hands on my face and kissed me. 'I think we're safe.'

The others fell asleep: we stayed up all night and watched the sunrise together. The birds went a little crazy beforehand, swirling and chirping in the navy blue sky. I closed my eyes, and leaned against him, the tiredness beginning to weigh my head down at last.

'Are you really going to wait around for me?' Wolfie asked.

'Hm?' I said, not opening my eyes.

'I suppose it's just started to occur to me that you may meet someone in the summer and forget what you feel about me right now,' Wolfie said, sort of smiling, but without a trace of a joke in his voice. 'And I suppose it's just started to occur to me that I'm quite worried about that.'

'Don't!' I said, amazed. 'I won't! You know how much I care about you.'

'Yeah, sometimes I just have a hard time believing you're for real,' Wolfie whispered. 'You're the sweetest, cleverest, kindest person I've ever met. I don't want to take any risk that might end up with me losing you. And I've signed up to this summer work without really thinking about that risk, and now I'm scared, and I feel like an idiot for not worrying enough about this before and for being so selfish and, even though I've worried about leaving *you* alone for the summer, I'm actually wondering now how I'm going to make it through four months without you.'

'The time, you know, it'll go like *that*,' I said, sleepily trying to snap my fingers, but just making them brush together.

'Come here,' he said, letting me curl up against his chest, holding me in both his arms, so I felt warm and safe and loved. When I woke up, I was in the same place, and Wolfie was awake, his lips resting on my forehead.

Chapter 18

Our goodbye at the airport was much more stressful than our last night together. I was no more than a muscle away from crying at any time; Wolfie was tired and worried that he'd forgotten things; Chunk was late; we were all running around, panicking, trying to be normal with each other and failing. Chunk's parents were there seeing him off and had given me and Wolfie a lift to the airport. But Wolfie's dad hadn't come – he only had me. That meant, of course, that we could be drippy and romantic and hold on to each other and say all the right things. But he was more worried about going than he wanted to say, I could tell, and it was making him distracted and even distant. Sometimes he'd sort of catch himself while he was looking up at the flight information boards – then he'd turn back to look in my eyes and, without saying a word, wrap his arms around me so tightly that I could hardly breathe and kiss my forehead.

'Oh God, this is it,' Wolfie said, when there was no time left. 'Are you going to be OK?'

'You're the one I'm worried about,' I said. Each second felt like the last second; everything I said felt like the last thing I'd be able to say before he went.

He squeezed me again. 'I'm going to miss you so much.'

'Yes,' I said. It was all I could manage because I knew my voice would break.

'Please don't go off me,' he said.

'I won't,' I said, my voice tiny.

'Or forget me.'

'I won't.'

'I love you,' Wolfie said.

'I love you.'

'I don't want to stop holding you.'

'Don't stop,' I said.

When he went through the final gate, I was praying he'd look back at me one more time, that he wouldn't just keep on walking away. He turned, half smiled and then he was gone.

Out of the windows, I could see planes taking off – they looked so small and fragile, darting into the clouds and disappearing. One of them would be taking Wolfie all the way to the other side of the world. I pressed the heels of my freezing cold hands into my teary face to try to push the tears back in and tidy myself up a bit before I found

Chunk's parents, who were waiting to take me back home. They said nice things and made jokes about the two boys doing some real work for a change, but we were all sad, and I thought Chunk's mum looked as if she wanted to cry as well. She asked me if I was hungry and offered me a Kit-Kat, but I felt sick and couldn't imagine ever wanting to eat again. We'd started out very early that morning, and the tiredness and hungriness and teariness together made me feel cold and drained and paper-thin. After about twenty minutes, Chunk's dad turned the radio on and we drove most of the rest of the way without speaking. My mind flashed images of Wolfie's face, like a photograph album of his smiles. He's gone, I thought.

I was feeling quite numb when I got home and my mum gave me a hug and asked if I was OK.

'I'm fine,' I said. 'I think it hasn't really sunk in yet.'

But that night I took a bath and cried, because he'd been able to leave me when we'd only just found each other, and I wondered how many things we'd let life put between us. I also cried happy tears, because I'd never felt so safe and loved before and, even though we wouldn't be together for months, I would feel that way again. I checked my e-mail, where there was usually some romantic, goofy note from Wolfie on it by the time I went to bed, but

there was only a note from Matty, saying she hoped I was
OK and that I should call her if I wanted to talk. I knew
I'd feel better hearing her voice, but it was easier to just
crawl into bed and sleep away the sadness – and I fell
asleep surprisingly quickly.

My family were brilliant over the next few days, because
I was being sort of ridiculous. I moped, I watched non-
stop reality TV and played all the songs that had meant
things to Wolfie and me, and tried to sing them meaning-
fully when I was alone. After my initial lost appetite, I
found I was perfectly able to eat whole packets of Jaffa
cakes in one sitting. I was bored and lonely, and I sometimes lay on my bed staring at the ceiling thinking, I was
happy before I met Wolfie, too – what did I do, then?
What did I do with my days? I had to quickly learn to
stop thinking about how I was going to fit every day
around Wolfie, and remember not to waste what I'd
previously thought of as the best time of the year. There
was no pressure from work and the weather was great. I
was, actually, sort of embarrassed about admitting to how
sad I was without him. I thought everyone might think I
was down for no real reason, and that they'd assure me
the time would pass quickly, while secretly thinking I was
being a bit wimpy.

What actually happened was that my family were sensitive and took my unhappiness seriously. They all seemed to be looking out for me and trying to cheer me up. My brother started forcing me to come and watch him and his mates playing in football matches, and my mum took me shopping and tried to buy me nice things, and my dad called me Tessie, the way he had when I was tiny, and took me to the pictures. I ended up growing closer to all of them that summer than I had been in years. I felt I was undergoing a real transformation, growing up.

But it was tough, right from the beginning. Wolfie e-mailed sooner than I'd expected. The good news was that there were lots of Internet cafés in Lima, but the bad news was that he wouldn't be staying in Lima. He wouldn't be too far from there, though, and hoped to be able to make regular-ish contact. Although he and Chunk had spent several weeks with Adam, organising their flights and accommodation, the exam period had been equally fraught and busy. There was a sense that he and Chunk had just trusted Adam to set everything up without really knowing every detail about what they'd be doing and how their days would be filled. He was just beginning to find out in proper detail what would be involved, and he kept me up to date as he did. He called every night for the first few nights to tell me he was excited to be there and missed me. He was using a cheap phone card that meant there was a lot of time-delay and echo on the line. Until we got used to it, we talked over each other all the time, and I repeated a lot of things that I thought he hadn't heard, only to hear my own voice saying them back twice a couple of seconds later, sounding annoying and high-pitched.

Just under a fortnight after he'd gone, a letter arrived by post. There was something about old-fashioned written letters that made them very special and important, even though he'd already talked to me on the phone about everything he'd written. He mostly e-mailed rather than writing letters because the Internet was so quick, and he made it to web cafés fairly regularly. I knew how much he loved getting my mails, so I sent a lot – there was usually a pile-up of about twenty short notes by the time he got to them, that all said the same sort of thing – that I missed him like mad – or talked about incredibly mundane things like TV programmes – stuff that must have made me sound like an idiot considering how he was spending his summer. His e-mails talked a lot about how sad he was without me, and how little free time he had, and how hard he was finding it to settle in, but at the same time he was genuinely enthusiastic and full of excitement about everything he was doing.

'I'm blown away by how beautiful it is. Every day. I

have to come back and see it properly with my girl,' he said to me on the phone.

'That's me, is it?' I said, glowing with pleasure.

'Yeah. You're my girl,' and I could hear the smile in his voice.

The out-of-date paper letters kept coming, although they were much less frequent than the e-mails. But he tried to send one a week, and I treasured them. They were longer and more detailed, because he wrote them in bed when he had lots of time and wasn't on the way to anywhere. One said he wasn't managing to find many vegetarian options – I knew this was no longer a problem – and talked in great detail about the night he and Chunk had spent in a weird little hotel with no locks on the doors. They'd woken up in the middle of the night to find a strange woman in the room with them, standing at the bottom of their beds, and both screamed, but later laughed at how scared they'd been. They were now staying with a friend of Adam's in a little village near Manchay, and in the daytime helping repair a children's home that had been completely destroyed by floods. Neither of them had any building experience, and, as Wolfie reminded me, they'd found it a struggle to put up a tent. The building manager therefore put them in charge of filling wheelbarrows with sand and going to fetch things.

'Guess what,' one letter said, 'I found a place that developed photos, and I got through a reel quickly. In a country with some of the most stunning views in the world, it seems a bit unfair of me to also send you a not-so-great looking one.'

I was expecting something sad: he'd sent me a dozen or so photographs in the folded sheets of paper. But as I looked through them there was nothing bad. There were beautiful views of mountains with a crazy blue sky, others of palm trees and stunning buildings, pyramids of oranges in a street market, a gorgeous, ornamental cathedral. When I saw the last picture I realised what his letter had been referring to and laughed out loud: it was Wolfie in a little hotel room, holding up a hand-written sign that said, *I love you*, and looking at me with big sad eyes. I knew he sort of meant it as a joke, with his over-the-top mournful expression and sad little sign, but I touched his face with my finger and looked at it for hours and loved it, because I didn't have many pictures of him.

I showed the photos to Matty. She was making an extra special effort not to leave me out while she and Jim were doing fun coupley things and we still spent a lot of time alone together, the way we always had. I wanted to share some of Wolfie's messages and stories with her, because somehow, if people knew that the romance was still happening between us, it made him seem more real, more mine, still officially my boyfriend and not just someone I talked to mostly online. Matty and I still watched the same trashy, romantic movies, and did absolutely nothing useful with our holiday, much to her mum's annoyance. We'd been given book lists for A-level English, for instance, and could have made a start on them. But it was hard to begin new things when we'd been working for so long and so hard on our exams and while we still waited anxiously for the results.

Lima is six hours behind Britain, which meant that to do realtime e-mailing I often had to stay up late, because Wolfie was working all day. The work sounded incredibly tough, but I could tell he was loving it.

'Physical labour is making me so fit,' he wrote me in one e-mail, 'You remember how puny I used to be? Weedy veggie? Get this, they let me do some of the brick-work today. You wait till you see me – you're going to have a boyfriend as good-looking as you. I am *hot*. And if you think *I'm* hot – which you will – wait till you get a load of Chunk. Three weeks off the PlayStation 'n' pies regime has turned him into a dude. *Tsssss!*'

Even over e-mail, he made me laugh.

While they worked, the children would sit around

and watch. They asked Chunk and Wolfie about Britain and what children were like there. Wolfie sent photographs of the ones he'd made friends with. They were absolutely adorable – shiny hair and beautiful, dark eyes. There was one picture I loved with Chunk being practically squashed by a group of small boys, laughing as they bounced on him. In some of the pictures, Peru looked like heaven, with big leafy plants and sunshine everywhere, while others showed the dusty sparseness of the shanty towns, and children with sad smiles and scared faces. Wolfie's photographs were incredible – sensitive and human and moving.

The A-level results came out first. My friends had all done pretty well, getting the right grades. Wolfie called me that morning, even though it would have been incredibly early for him, to tell me how he'd done. Chunk's dad had woken them up, and then he'd called his dad, who, he said, had been waiting for a more sociable hour to call him. As far as his university requirements went – they wanted three Cs – he was a grade down in maths (D) but two grades up in history – he got an A – and one grade up in French. But since he was going to defer entry, he said, it probably wouldn't matter if Liverpool didn't take him, because he could reapply next year. He said he and

Chunk were going out to celebrate. I went out with Jane and Lara a couple of nights later, and they were telling me how excited and nervous they were about leaving home. I felt sad and shivery, and young. No matter how close we'd become, there were some things I couldn't do along with them and the differences kept us a little distant. And the next morning Wolfie had sent me an e-mail to tell me the two girls had called him and Chunk when they got in, and he realised how much they were missing by being away – how many important moments. He seemed quite sad, and it hurt me that I couldn't hold him and tell him everything was OK, that everything was great. It would be a lie, but I needed to hear *someone* saying it.

From: wolfiec@globernet.com

To: ttaylor@spectraweb.com

Subject: Re: Re: I miss you

Last night Adam brought us back a bottle of Pisco — which is an incredibly strong wine. We drank a couple of shots and got a bit drunk and talked about girls. Chunk said he'd always been in love with Jane. Ad talked about the girl he'd been living with all of last year, who left him two months ago. I didn't have a sob story. But I'm having a harder time than

both of them, because they don't have someone
they miss and who isn't with them.

Love, W

I got almost all As in my GCSEs. One A* in English, and a B in Drama. It was better than I'd been expecting, and I was pretty delighted and so were my family. Matty got more A*s, but more Bs, in her science and language subjects. For a long time, I had thought this would be the most important day in my life, but, when it happened, I'd already seen someone I loved getting his A-level results, and I was thinking more about the fact that I'd be able to call him that night and wouldn't have to tell him any sad news. My mum knew how excited I was and, since I was using a special dial-up number that let me talk for four pence a minute, she let me talk to him practically all evening. One of my friends was having a party, but I knew I'd have spent the whole thing waiting to get home to speak to him, so I didn't go. Matty tried hard to talk me into it, but I knew what I was doing. Sometimes when you're sad, or dreading a party, you can get caught up in the spirit of it, and your mood will lift, and you'll forget everything for a while. But if you go there knowing you'd rather be somewhere else, you'll keep thinking about that thing. After shouting about how delighted he was with my results, Wolfie told me off, and said I shouldn't be skipping parties and missing things just to talk to him. But then we just talked and talked and talked, and I knew I'd made the right choice.

From: wolfiec@globernet.com

To: ttaylor@spectraweb.com

Subject: exclusive scoop!

Congratulations again on your brilliant brain. I'm now worried that you're mentally correcting the grammar in my e-mails.

Yes, my GCSE Spanish is helping me out. I can understand a lot of what people say, but I'm very slow at speaking to them. Luckily they're very patient.

Lots of volunteers are Peruvian themselves — there's a culture of selflessness, which is surprising and really makes you think. But the kids here are often in real need of a bit of love. We took some into Lima — with permission — and to an ice cream parlour. Excellent ice cream. I showed them a picture of you — they said you were beautiful.

Sending you photos of kids with ice cream

smeared on their faces. I wish you were here to
see it and hear them giggle.

From: wolfiec@globernet.com

To: ttaylor@spectraweb.com

Subject: xxxxxxxxxxxxx

i love you.

I hadn't had a boyfriend before. I'd been happy before.
Why, then, was it so difficult being so far from Wolfie,
when he sent me e-mails, talked to me on the phone at least
once a week, and I knew he was coming back? For one
thing, the way I'd lived before, staying in watching telly,
surfing websites, eating vast quantities of Jaffa cakes, now
seemed totally boring. But it was more than that. Scarier. I
had more to worry about and more to lose. I was afraid
that the separation might change him. He was really living
now – going out and doing important and amazing things,
meeting new people. While I was excited for him and loved
hearing about it, how was I going to compete with that
kind of excitement, and what was going to keep him in our
dull, tiny town for the rest of the year? If I was the only
thing keeping him here, would I be enough?

But it was summer, so it was impossible to be sad every day

when the weather was so gorgeous. One day, Matty and I were lying in my back garden enjoying the sun. Matty said, 'Remember when I told you love was the last thing we wanted, and then we both went straight out and got it.'

'I know – it's nuts. Have you changed your mind?'

'Well, Jim's in our year, so I've put off one of the problems for a couple of years.'

'I think now that you've found Jim, you've put off all of the problems.'

Matty turned on to her stomach, and looked at me. 'I think I was a bit addicted to worrying,' she said. 'It's a bit unnerving, all this happiness. Jim never strops, he never tells me off, he never whines about me not giving him enough attention. Where's the catch? He just makes everything easy, and I can't see a time when he won't.'

'Wolfie makes everything hard, I think,' I said. 'He tells me he loves me, then he tells me he won't spend the summer with me. But I'm only unhappy because I'm happy, you know? If I didn't get so much out of going out with him, if thinking about him didn't make me smile every single time, then it wouldn't make me so sad to not have him around. So it's not real unhappiness, is it? It's just noticing that there are other . . . emotions . . . than being in love.'

'Yeah,' Matty said, 'I've heard there are. But what's the point of them?

Chapter 19

I could see Wolfie even though he was only talking to me on the phone. See him clearly. Almost touch him. I could see the light stubble on his cheeks and chin, the softness of his mouth. He was wearing the army-green T-shirt I loved and the cords he'd worn the first time we kissed, and he was holding the phone and talking to me, like I was watching a film of him, but for some reason I couldn't answer him back – I couldn't speak. He was saying, 'Tess, I can't live without you any longer. This whole summer's pointless without you; Peru is beautiful, but I miss you too much. I'm going to get a boat back in the morning and we can be together. We never have to be apart again and I'm not going anywhere without you again.' I was still trying to answer, and couldn't. I could only hold the receiver more tightly and look at him, my eyes pleading with him, but that seemed to be enough. He was saying, 'Me too. I'm *always* going to be in love with you,' then, almost shouting, 'I'm always going to love you, Tessa,' and getting further away, his voice getting quieter and the image of him fading and shrinking, and he was kissing his fingertips and blowing gently on them, while his brown eyes searched for me and found me.

It was a dream; I was dreaming. My bedroom was drenched with sunshine – the curtains were rubbish at keeping the light out. It was only 6.20 a.m. and I didn't have to get up or go anywhere. Wolfie had been gone for sixty-four days, and would be in Peru for another sixty-five. He'd e-mailed to say he'd bought a new phone card and would be calling tonight to use it all, to mark the halfway point.

It had been days since the last time he'd phoned me, and not hearing from him was hard. But when he called it was hard too, because, when it was over, or after I'd read the e-mails he sent over an Internet session, I knew there would be nothing else until at least the next day. The dream was bitter-sweet, because I missed him so much it almost felt like *something*, but I'd woken too soon and couldn't catch it back.

I got up anyway, tiptoeing downstairs to make myself a cup of tea and listen to the birdsong. It was strange being the only person up when the house was light. I read yesterday's newspaper at the kitchen table, picking the cold icing off a cake I'd found in the fridge. Today Matty and I were going to sort out her mum's garden.

Matty wasn't really up by the time I got round to hers.

She was still wearing her pyjamas and watching MTV.

'Come and look at this,' she said, turning the volume up on a video she liked.

'Aren't you two going to do something useful, today?' Matty's mum said, walking past the door. 'You go back to school the day after tomorrow and you haven't done anything with your summer, and, Matilda, you're not at all prepared for going back – you haven't started organising anything. You shouldn't waste your free time. It's precious, you know.'

Matty rolled her eyes. We ended up watching music videos for the next hour, without Matty making much of a move to get up. She was telling me about how Jim was turning out to be the best boyfriend she'd ever had; he was so romantic and cute.

'When you started going out with Wolfie,' Matty said, 'I realised there was probably something wrong with me and Lee. That was probably why I was suspicious of Wolfie – he sounded too good to be true. I know relationships are always easier at the start, and you start taking each other for granted a bit, but Lee was never . . . you know. Jim doesn't just get me – he *cares* about me. I don't think I've had a boy like that before.'

I was so pleased for her. Matty's looks and confidence had always guaranteed her no shortage of boys, but all too often they'd been the wrong types of boy – some of them, like Lee, were insecure and tried to put her down, so she wouldn't realise she was too good for them, others had mainly been interested in her because she was so pretty. Jim had always loved her, the real her; the proof was in Cadeby Wood. Matty was showing me the little pretend sleeve-notes he'd written in the case of a CD he'd made her, when her mum came in and said my mum was outside in the car.

I was instantly worried. I knew there was no non-serious reason she'd choose to drive over when I had my phone. I hurried downstairs, trying to work out what could be wrong, and why she'd drive here without just calling and asking me to go back. I was afraid it was something terribly serious, that maybe my brother or my dad were hurt, and my heart started beating out of control.

'Tessa, I need to talk to you,' she said when I got to the car. Her voice was horribly low and quiet. Her face was pale and she looked afraid, which really frightened me, because I couldn't remember ever having seen her like that. I sort of waved to Matty, who stood in her doorway, looking concerned, trying to reassure her that I was fine even though I didn't have a clue what was wrong. I got in the car and Mum drove a little way around the corner, away from the houses, and parked.

'Chunk called our house just a little while ago. Wolfie was in a traffic accident. He died yesterday.'

I believed her straight away and it sank in straight away and I started hurting straight away, and my mum leaned over me in the car, hugging me and stroking my hair while I shook. I was shivering all over; my skin was hurting, and I thought I might forget how to breathe. I could hear my voice, high and weird sounding – it didn't sound like me. It sounded as if I could hear it through speakers, ringing in my ears and making fun of me. I kept asking the same questions: 'Do they know it's true? Is it definitely Wolfie? Do they KNOW? Is he definitely dead? Has Chunk seen him?' But I was just hoping I could find a loophole that would make it not have happened, while in my heart I knew there was no hope. It was almost like I understood all at once why our separation had been so hard – why I'd been afraid for us when he said he had to go – as if I'd somehow known something bad would happen.

He'd been crossing a road in Lima, when a lorry was taking a corner too fast and lost control; it crashed through a shop window after hitting Wolfie. They told me he would have died instantly.

* * *

Chunk travelled straight back to Britain. He came to visit me the next day, and brought round some of Wolfie's things – his wallet, his hoodie that I sometimes used to wear, some photographs of Manchay he'd just had developed. There weren't many of him, they were all of Peruvian children and pretty views and Chunk, and I felt bad as I looked through them, because I was disappointed there weren't more pictures of Wolfie.

'He was nuts about you, you know,' Chunk said, mumbling, because he wasn't used to being serious. I looked at him: he looked terrible – his eyes were bloodshot and his hair was dirty and sticking up all over. 'He kept complaining every night before we slept about having to share a bedroom with me. The morning it happened, he woke up and said he'd just been dreaming about seeing you. Sorry, that's sort of a stupid thing to say, but I remember it.'

'I just like hearing about him,' I said.

'He was missing you a lot,' Chunk said. 'He liked the work, but he got quite blue in the evenings. Wouldn't join in when I was trying to pull local girls. You know, typical man in love.'

I started crying, and Chunk put his arms around me and I let myself fall against him, even though we'd never really touched before. I buried my face in his shoulder, drenching it with tears, gulping with pain. In a moment of quiet, I heard Chunk sniff and realised he was crying too. He'd just lost his best friend. He'd had to fly back alone, knowing that he'd never see him again. Then he'd come straight to me. He was amazingly brave and kind, and I loved him and wished there was something I could do to thank him and make him feel better.

When Chunk went home, I put the hoodie around my shoulders and curled into a ball on my bed, burying my face deep in the sheets so I could cry out loud without anyone hearing me and worrying that I was dying, although it felt as if I might, and I wanted to, at that moment I really wanted to. I felt as though my heart had been ripped straight out of my body, leaving a raw, aching hole in me. This horrible, *physical* pain.

In Wolfie's wallet, there was a black and white photograph of me laughing that I realised was the one he'd taken when we went to the wood together for the newspaper piece. On the back of it he'd written, '*Tess, ten minutes before we first kissed*'.

When school started again, my mum let me take the first week off; we'd agreed it would just be a week. I'd expected her to make me go, and to tell me it would be good for me to get out and into a new routine, that it would take my mind off things. Instead, she made me jammy toast, and my dad took over all the rest of the cooking, and, when she had time, my mum sat with me and held me, and sometimes she cried too.

Wolfie's funeral was on the first Friday after school started again and, as I hadn't been back to school yet, and had hardly stepped outside my house, I found the large group of people made me nervous, and I wanted to hide from them. Wolfie's mum and dad sat together and spent ages talking to each other, which I found touching. Chunk talked about his best friend in front of everyone. I didn't. I couldn't. During the service, Jane held my hand and cried the most. Matty sat on my other side and leaned against me.

Wolfie's mum came over to talk to me at the wake. She looked a lot like him; she had the same swingy brown hair, the same brown eyes, but hers were sadder, and harder.

'He wrote to me to tell me he'd fallen in love,' Wolfie's mum said. She had asked me to call her by her first name, Chloe. 'He sounded happier than I've ever known him being.'

'He *was* happy,' I said. I wanted to tell her how fantastic her son was. But I didn't really dare, because I was afraid of her. I was afraid that she might suddenly shout at me and tell me off for letting him go to Peru. A small part of me was almost angry with her for having hurt him. I knew that the pain she was going through must have been awful, and she must have felt so much guilt. In the end, though, I realised all I wanted to tell her was that he had been happy.

Chapter 20

The next morning, Lara called from her mobile to ask if I wanted to go to Cadeby Wood with her and Jane and Chunk. My parents were having breakfast and I told them where I was going. My dad asked me if I was OK, and I nodded, and then as I was leaving the kitchen he said, 'Come here, Tessie,' and pulled me close and hugged me. He didn't say anything else.

I met Jane and Lara at the end of my street and we walked quietly into the Wood together. It was a little before nine o'clock and it was going to be a beautiful day. There was a slight chill in the air and the sky was a very pale blue and completely clear. The wood was rustling with wildlife hurrying to hide from the daytime visitors, and there was a warm, leafy smell. It was everything I loved most about it, without the one person who had made it my favourite place on earth. Chunk found us sitting in a line on the trunk of a fallen tree, and sat down in silence with us.

'Can you feel him?' Jane said. 'I feel like he's here.'

I wished it could be true. I wished that he was there,

in every tree that leaned, breathing, towards us, in the squirrels that circled their roots, in the rays of sunshine filtering through the heavy leaves that had already started turning golden brown. That he could see me here, loving him, waiting for him, and send his love back to me.

The others told stories about him. Lara talked about the first time he had brought her to the Wood, when she hadn't known it existed, and that that was when she'd found out why he was called Wolfie. Jane remembered how the four of them once got a group detention, because Wolfie had accidentally broken a table trying to get Jane's diary down from a high window ledge where a boy who was bullying Jane had thrown it, and they'd all agreed to take the blame together but not to grass on the bully. I was desperate to hear more about him – I wanted to know *everything*. But at the same time, even though these people were my friends, and they meant so much to me and wanted to talk about how much they loved Wolfie, I couldn't stop myself being jealous of them for knowing him better than me. They had enjoyed so much time with him – and I'd had so little. I hated myself for feeling like that, but it pounded through my head every time they finished each other's sentences and smiled at the memories. It didn't seem fair, when I'd believed I would spend for ever getting to know everything about him, that I would only have a few months' worth of memories to last me the rest of my life. Then Jane told a story about the first time he told them all that he was falling for me, and said she'd never known him like that, so shy and serious. It was as if she had read my mind and wanted to reassure me that I knew a Wolfie they hadn't known, too. Then Chunk said some more about the way Wolfie talked about me in Peru, and I was embarrassed and moved by their kindness, and just incredibly grateful for their friendship.

On my first day back at school, I felt, or knew, that everyone was looking at me. I was terrified that at any moment anything might make me lose it, and the last thing I wanted to do was to cry in front of everyone and attract more attention. But when people were kind, and felt sorry for me, it was almost impossible not to cry, and I seemed to spend the whole day trying to draw my face back into itself and not let go. To keep the tears in my eyes, because, if one escaped, there would be nothing to stop me breaking down completely.

I slipped away at lunch-time to sit by the goat's pen. Matty came along to ask if I wanted her to get me something from outside school, but she could sense I wanted to be alone.

'Do you remember him?' I asked the goat, when I

was sure that no one was anywhere near. 'He helped you once. He let you see a little more of the world. Just for a brief moment.' I knew that if anyone saw me or heard me they'd think I might be losing my mind. I needed to speak out loud but not to be heard by anyone who could say something back to me, or tell me I'd be fine. I didn't want to hear it, because I knew it was a lie.

The week went on and being at school did help, in a way. I was forced to think about coursework and timetables and where I was supposed to be, and to use my brain to worry about other things. I couldn't just follow Matty around in a daze, because we had different classes. I'd been crying for so long that it almost seemed like a break: being made to focus on words, writing, spending time not thinking about myself. I hadn't realised how much I'd needed the break until it came, but I also felt I didn't deserve it – that it was wrong and bad to begin to move on, no matter how small the move. Whenever my concentration ebbed and my mind fell back on Wolfie, I felt as though my heart had been temporarily emptied and was flooding again, fast, with sadness, and that it beat more heavily and pulsed with waves of guilt, as if I was letting him go, as if a few of the million threads that held him to me were breaking. And it hurt. It hurt so much.

It was deeper, more searing, completely different

from the pain I'd felt when he left me to go to Peru. All through the summer, there had been aching and longing and fear for him and me – but always hope. There were e-mails to read and the real sound of his voice when he called, not just a memory. There was more of him, or the promise of more in the future. I knew that I could count the moments until I felt happy again, no matter how brief the conversations and e-mails were – no matter how quickly sadness would follow, or the loneliness start to pull the ground from under my feet. Now, there was nothing to stop me falling, and no one to catch me.

Epilogue

Matty said that I have nothing to worry about. 'Yeah, not much,' I said. I'd been crying again, and I had my hair in front of my red streaky face, and was resting my chin on my hands on the edge of the sofa.

She brushed my hair off my forehead and smiled.

'You?' she said. 'I don't need to worry about you. You're Tess.'

'Lucky me,' I said.

'Listen, you twit,' Matty said. 'Not once in your whole life have you settled for anything. Not once have you wasted your time with anyone who didn't deserve you or anyone you didn't think was the coolest person alive. You've always had that, but you used to worry that you'd never fall in love. And now you've fallen in love.'

'Exactly. I had my chance. I didn't settle. I waited for the right guy and the right guy is gone.'

'Which *means*,' Matty said, 'that in addition to having the kind of pride that means you don't settle for losers and idiots and *Lees*, you know you have the ability to fall head over heels, check your e-mail three hundred times a day, burst out laughing when you're walking down the street because you're so happy you met him, in TRUE LOVE!'

'There was only him,' I said.

'No,' Matty said. 'I'm not going to tell you you'll meet another man like him, because I know that Wolfie was unique. But he is *not* the only man you'll ever be in love with. Your heart has already proved to you that it works. The people you should worry about are the people who've never been in love. Like my mum – I think she always did what was sensible and never really lost herself. I never saw her kiss my dad, or light up when he walked in, the way I sometimes see your mum look at your dad, or the way I know I look at Jim. There are some people, I think, who just don't *feel* that. You know, who just never fall that hard. You fall all the way, you're one of the lucky ones.' She leaned back and took a sip of her latte. 'So no, I don't worry about you. So you shouldn't either.'

I don't know if I can believe her. When they talk in songs and movies about broken hearts, I understand. That's how it feels to me – that I'm broken, that I'll never know how to be really, purely happy again, the way I was before. But if someone offered me the chance to turn back time and take away Wolfie from my life, so I didn't have the pain I've been feeling since he died, I'd tell them where to stick it. I'd get angry. My months with Wolfie are the most important of my life, and I still have them, and I always will. The person I'm learning to be started life with him – he helped me to understand myself, to listen to my heart, to listen to other people more than worrying about what they think of me. He's a part of me for ever.

It's when I look at the pictures he took that I see how important that is, and can almost believe people when they tell me I was lucky to be there when he was there, for however long. The warmth and happiness in the eyes of the children he photographed tells some of the story of what an amazing person he was, how caring and sensitive and passionate. Seeing the effect he had on other people and knowing he chose me to love is the greatest joy in my life.

This morning, I got a letter from Wolfie's mum.

Tessa,

Thank you so much for your letter and the pictures. They broke my heart and made me happy at the same time. I felt humbled by the overwhelming love and affection for him that I saw in Wolfie's friends at the funeral. I regret not having spent more time with my beautiful son. I hope he knew how much I loved him.

I've enclosed a letter Wolfie sent me a little while ago. While I treasure everything he gave me, this one, I think, belongs to you.

With my very best wishes,

Chloe

Dear Chloe

I hope you're all doing well up in Glasgow, and that the Scottish sun is starting to burn a hole through the rain clouds.

Tessa, the girl I mentioned in my last letter, is now my girlfriend. Can you believe it? She's amazing. She's beautiful and clever and funny and she doesn't think I'm a jerk. But she's also incredibly kind and sensitive, and has no idea how amazing she is. When I wake up in the morning and remember *that she's my girl, I think I must be the luckiest guy in the world. Did I mention that she's beautiful? We've been spending all our spare time together; we went to Bridlington last week and I took a photograph of her by the sea (it's enclosed – isn't she gorgeous? She hates being photographed). I wish you could meet her – you'd fall in love with her too. I know your schedule makes it hard for you to come down to England very often, but if you're thinking about it in the near future, for whatever reason, do give us a shout and we'll all have a cup of coffee or something. I'm just so proud of her and want to show her off to everyone.*

Give my best to Angus and Sasha and Hannah and April.

I love you, Mum.

David